CHAPTER 1

CAMPBELL CASTLE, ARGYLLSHIRE, SCOTLAND, 1307

"You must take a bride, Cameron! You're baron now of a great estate, Seoras MacDougall rotting in his grave, the devil take him. Never again will the Campbells swear allegiance tae that accursed clan, so the quicker you marry and produce a son and heir, the better—och, nephew, are you listening tae me?"

Cameron grimaced at his barrel-chested uncle's bluster, Torence Campbell striding back and forth in front of the massive fireplace at the middle of the great hall.

Aye, he was listening. How could he not be with such a clamor? His head ached from the same words he'd heard for the past four days—God help him.

You must take a bride! You must take a bride!

Was it only four days since Robert the Bruce had named Cameron as baron of the most formidable fortress in all of Argyllshire?

Four days since his closest friend and former commander, Gabriel MacLachlan, had slain Seoras and then returned to his own castle as a baron no longer, but elevated to an earl?

Both he and Gabriel rewarded beyond any expectation by King Robert for saving his life—och, Cameron had only done what came as naturally to him as breathing, which was wielding a sword. He and Conall, his younger brother, and Gabriel had fought side by side as warriors for one overlord or another since their youth, all of them younger sons with little hope of inheriting land or title.

Yet Gabriel had become a laird upon the death of his elder brother—murdered by one of Seoras's henchmen, they had discovered as well only days ago—and now Cameron was the laird of the newly named Campbell Castle, a blessing that had begun to feel as much a curse.

Especially now when Uncle Torence raised his clenched fist and roared so loudly that the rafters seemed to shake.

"I wish it had been me tae save King Robert's life! I would have wedded and bedded a lass that very day tae honor our clan—"

"I doubt Aunt Agatha would appreciate such a gesture," Cameron said tightly, rising from his chair to tower over his uncle, "and *dinna* utter a word tae me again of honor. Is it not enough for now that the MacDougalls have been defeated? Is it not enough for now that the castle prison has been emptied—Campbells among them? You said you wanted tae speak tae me and you've had your say. I'll take a bride when I'm ready and only then!"

Cameron pushed past his uncle, a clutch in his chest from a declaration he had never uttered before even as Torence shouted behind him.

"When do you think that might be? The Campbell himself sent me here and demands an answer! Our chieftain and your own cousin. You're not an island, Cameron, no matter this fortress and its lands. Our kinsmen and allies expect much of you—"

"Enough, Uncle, I heard your howling all the way out in the bailey," came Conall's voice as he strode into the great hall and flashed a reassuring grin at Cameron. "Give me a moment with my brother and then I'll join you for a cup of ale."

Cameron scowled back at him, his patience at an end with all this discourse of brides and wedding and bedding.

He was a man like any other, the sight of a bonny lass more than enough to stir his loins. Yet that felt like a curse, too, for his wretched shyness around women had made him avoid them at all costs for as long as he could remember.

Only once as a lad had he attempted to approach a girl with a wilting fistful of wildflowers, the memory a painful one even now. He had become so tongue-tied that she had laughed at him and thrown his gift into the dirt and stomped upon it, which had made him vow to never again suffer such humiliation.

Even Conall knew to this day not to tease him or prod him, and Cameron had walloped any man who had dared to question his reticence when it came to the fairer sex.

Aye, he was untried and untested in the bedchamber, but what of it? His younger brother by two years had more than made up for Cameron's lack of carnal experience, the two of them as unlike in that regard as night and day.

"She's married," he said dryly, reading Conall's mind and catching him by the arm as a buxom maidservant hurried past them with a stack of freshly laundered linens.

"Truly?" Conall gave him a roguish smile, his gaze never leaving the young woman's equally ample backside. "A marvel of God's handiwork, aye, brother? I'd say from that saucy wink she gave me that she has no hus-

3

band—or surely not one that pleases her. You've always had an eye for details, Cameron, but I'm astonished that you would know such facts already about the servants—"

"She wears a silver ring on her finger, did you not see it?" Swearing low under his breath, Cameron let go of Conall's arm and faced him. "Did you not come tae find me for some reason?"

Conall nodded, his good humor hardly abated at Cameron's gruff tone.

They might have been twins for how closely they resembled each other, with their midnight black hair, deep blue eyes, and near equal height and muscular girth, but their temperaments couldn't be more dissimilar. Even now Conall still grinned while Cameron felt his scowl deepen and his jaw tighten with impatience.

"Oh, aye, I came tae warn you, Laird Campbell."

"Warn me?"

"Indeed. Word has flown that two daughters of the clan—distant cousins, mind you—will be arriving this afternoon tae make your acquaintance. A messenger just arrived from our chieftain himself—"

"Blast and damn! Will my whole life be ordered now that I'm a landed baron? Four days past, I answered tae no one but Gabriel—our existence of no more notice tae our kinsmen than a flea biting a hound's ear. Aye, renowned warriors, both of us, but what of that? Always one battle away from drawing our last breath and with no use for hearth or family—and then... *this*!"

Conall ducked as Cameron swung his arm to indicate the impressive great hall that had been stripped of any shields and banners of the MacDougalls and adorned instead with those of Clan Campbell.

Clan Campbell.

Nothing of his own, *Cameron Campbell*, but already he had commissioned a banner and painted shield to place above the ornately carved chair where he would sit as ruling baron of this strategic fortress.

Aye, still a warrior, but so much more—och, Robert the Bruce must have lost his senses to award him so much and so soon.

Already the king had left with his forces enlarged in number, thanks to his foray into Argyll, and returned to Dumbarton to prepare for King Edward's expected invasion of Scotland. He had commanded Cameron, Gabriel, Conall, and other men loyal to him to remain behind and ensure Argyll remained under his sovereignty.

That weighty charge meant training the men now under his command—former prisoners and eager young kinsmen who had flocked to the fortress to take up arms under Cameron—so that they would be ready to fight when the need arose.

Clearly, from his disheveled hair and sweaty tunic, Conall had been hard at his new duties, which were to whip the men into shape as quickly as possible.

He loved to fight as much as he loved women, life sometimes seeming a game to him that Robert the Bruce must have recognized. The king had promised a reward to Conall, too, for helping to save his life— though he'd said he needed some time to think upon it before any pronouncement was made. Conall hadn't seemed to mind at all, but had shrugged and laughed, just as he chuckled now and clapped Cameron on the back.

"Ease yourself, brother. The Campbell doesna rule you, and he knows how highly King Robert esteems you. It's strategy, pure and simple—chess pieces tae be moved upon the board. Always remember that you're in charge here, no matter our clansmen trying tae influence you. There's no harm in meeting the lasses—"

"Och, God." Cameron set off with determined strides toward the archway leading out to the bailey, that same clutch in his chest as Conall hastened after him.

His knuckles white as he gripped the hilt of his sword at his belt.

A fine sheen of sweat breaking out on his face... aye, he could feel it.

His tongue growing thick and heavy as if he already faced the young women who would soon be demanding his attention.

"Cameron!"

He ignored his brother and strode even faster, desperate now to do the only thing that had ever calmed him.

Wield his sword. Fight. Train.

Until he was so exhausted that he could barely stand, though he knew other responsibilities would call him away before he had a chance to reach that welcome state.

Battlements and fortifications to inspect alongside the Campbell kinsmen he'd named as his captains.

His newly appointed steward, Fergus, needing some of his time to discuss the domestic workings of the fortress.

The chief cook, Montrose—a Frenchman, for God's sake—come to plague him with pleas to make fancier meals of stuffed this or glazed that even though Cameron preferred plainer fare.

Farmers clamoring for time with him to discuss crops and cattle, villagers coming to him with their concerns, and the stout head of housekeeping, Berta, asking what else she could do to make him comfortable in his sumptuous suite of rooms in one of the square towers.

Did he want imported silken sheets upon his bed like Earl Seoras had insisted upon? Candles scented with lavender or thyme? Musicians to lull him to sleep at night with harp and lute? God help him, *what was he*?

A fearsome warrior or a wastrel to grow soft with ridiculous comfort and wretched excess?

"Cameron, wait!"

He had already stepped outside into blinding sunlight and a piercing blue sky—another fine, late spring day in a June that had proved warmer than most and needing more rain.

More worries! More concerns! He drew his sword and made his way toward the outer bailey filled with the grunting of men hard at training and metal ringing against metal—and already he felt his breathing grow calmer and his mind clearing.

Only then did he stop and turn to face Conall, who almost ran into him for how abruptly Cameron had turned around.

"*What*, brother?"

"I was going tae offer tae entertain our guests, if you'd like. The lasses are coming tae Campbell Castle whether you wish them here or not—"

"*Entertain?*" Now Cameron smiled wryly, though he felt no humor. "Lay a finger upon a one of them, Conall —stroke even a strand of hair and you'll find yourself wed so quickly that your teeth will rattle. Is that what you want? A wife?"

"Me? God, no. I thought only tae relieve you of a burden—aye, you've so much on your shoulders—"

"An irate father and outraged clan willna ease my burdens! I'll be sending them home as soon as they arrive, with the same answer I gave Uncle Torence—I'll take a bride only when I'm ready."

His throat tightened at the words, Cameron swallowed hard as he set out again, his brother's only answer to shrug and then come after him.

Cameron could hear him chuckling, Conall clearly unperturbed by his warning, which made him more resolute than ever to send his unwanted guests packing straightaway.

It amazed him to this day that Conall hadn't sired a dozen black-haired bastards, given his good-natured sway over women, but mayhap he knew some trick to avoid fatherhood though he'd sowed his oats far and wide.

By God, what did Cameron know of such fleshly mysteries? He had never asked for any insight and had no intention of doing so. Shoving the entire mess from his mind, he grasped his sword all the tighter and headed for the outer bailey—

"Laird Campbell, I must speak with you!"

Groaning, Cameron stopped as one of the guards from the prison rushed toward him, the stricken look upon the man's face causing him to stiffen.

"What is it, man?"

"We've found more captives, Laird! We thought all the cells emptied, just as you ordered, until a stench most foul in one of them seemed tae come from beneath the floor. We swept away the straw and found a trapdoor with a chamber underneath. Aye, and five men crammed into that wretched hole, well, what's left of them. Two dead and the others skin and bones—and one a youth, no more than sixteen, I'd wager—"

"By God, did you move them tae the infirmary?" Cameron cut him off, Conall having come up beside him. "Are they able tae speak? More Campbells?"

"No, Laird, they're Irish. So one of them claimed, the other two unconscious. We dinna know if they're friend or foe so we laid them out upon the cell floor and I came tae find you—"

"If they're prisoners of Seoras's, of course they're friends—probably come across the water tae fight for King Robert—enough! Take me tae them."

Scowling, Cameron didn't wait for the guard but strode ahead, calling out to Conall, "Didna you tell Uncle Torence you'd join him for a cup of ale? Go on, then, but meet me afterward at the training field."

Cameron didn't glance behind him to see if his brother had obliged him, for he knew Conall was highly disciplined when it came to orders—aye, well, except when it came to women.

Cursing under his breath, he wondered if the guards had called for the healer, Tobias, the man heavily tasked of late with all the freed prisoners.

Most had managed to stumble out of their filthy cells while unfortunate others knocked at death's door, damn Seoras to hell! Cameron wondered if they might find other cramped spaces beneath the prison floors. The thought sickened him and made him walk all the faster toward the stone building with narrow slits for windows at the far corner of the fortress—aye, far enough away so that those feasting in the great hall wouldn't hear the moans and screams.

A pair of guards bowed their heads in deference as Cameron approached and pushed open the heavy metal-studded door so he could enter. At once his eyes watered and he sucked in his breath, the stench of the place overwhelming.

He was accustomed to the smell of death after battle, but this wretched place seemed to reek of misery and despair, though not by his doing.

Seoras, during his short reign as earl, had filled the place to the rafters—and clearly beneath the floors— with most of the hapless prisoners destined for execution. Cameron's part in saving King Robert had spared them that fate, and there could be none more loyal than freed men with a second chance at life.

"Just ahead, Laird."

The Campbell guard had spoken behind him, Cameron's jaw tight as he turned from the dark hallway into a lamplit cell to see Tobias rising from a crouched position over what appeared a lifeless body. The stocky healer glanced at Cameron over his shoulder.

9

"Three dead, Laird Campbell, and those over there, barely alive."

Grateful that Tobias had been summoned, Cameron stared grimly at the two figures stretched out upon the straw... one so slight of form that he wondered if the lad might be younger than sixteen. The other male bore a graying beard, which amazed him that an older prisoner had survived, while the dead men, all younger as well, had perished.

Without a word, Tobias beckoned to the four menservants waiting just inside the cell, who stretched out blankets upon the straw to use as makeshift stretchers. Then he moved over to the nearest prisoner to lend a hand, his voice low and grave.

"Take the lass first—"

"*Lass?*" Dumbstruck, Cameron stared at Tobias, who nodded his balding head.

"Eighteen, nineteen, who can say? She's more than half dead from lack of food and water and likely will die this night—"

"Stand aside, *now*!"

Cameron didn't think, didn't hesitate, but moved to the slender figure and knelt down beside her, staring in disbelief.

Her face deathly pale. Short red hair plastered to her head. Thin arms and long legs telling him that she stood tall, aye, taller than most women—if she ever stood again.

"Lass?" Still incredulous, Cameron couldn't take his eyes from her hollow cheeks even as Tobias leaned down to press his palm to her forehead.

"Aye, Laird, and burning with fever. She'll die right here in this cell if I canna get her quickly tae the infirmary—och, be gentle with her."

Cameron already had picked her up from the floor, her weight so featherlight that indeed, she was no more than flesh and bones.

Her head lolled back.

One arm lodged against him while the other dangled limply, along with her legs... and what appeared now as Tobias lifted a lantern, her soiled face etched with what Cameron would swear were tracks of tears.

Tears...

CHAPTER 2

"Go, Tobias! Lead the way."

The healer murmured his assent and hastened from the cell, Cameron hard on his heels. He heard the menservants grunting as they lifted up the other prisoner, but his mind wasn't on the older man... just the lass.

An Irish lass. So the guard had told him, and Cameron intended to thoroughly question the man to learn if anything more had been said.

How could she not be Irish with that shock of red hair? Aye, matted and dirty, but still as bright a hue as any he'd seen. Yet clipped so short as if she had intended to pass as a youth, her dirty tunic, trousers, and leather shoes attesting to the ruse.

Cameron would never have guessed the truth if Tobias hadn't pointed it out to him, for she had no breasts to speak of—

"The infirmary is this way, Laird!" the healer's voice cut into his thoughts, but Cameron only shook his head.

"It's overrun with men—no fit place for a young woman," he said grimly, continuing past the wooden structure not far from the prison and toward the massive keep. "She'll have a room in one of the towers—"

"Laird, I've so many tae care for—the other freed prisoners, not tae have her close by..."

Tobias had fallen silent at the dark scowl Cameron cast him over his shoulder, which brooked no further discussion.

Though the healer was heavily built, Cameron still towered over him as he did with most men—except for Gabriel MacLachlan, who had him by a few inches. The two of them together on the battlefield had made even their most fearsome enemies quake in their boots.

"You'll have as many servants tae help you as you need—och, man, do you have all your potions and bottles in that basket slung over your arm? I can feel the fever burning like flame through her clothes."

"Not all, Laird, but it's enough for now," Tobias answered hastily, clearly chastened as he followed Cameron through the archway that led into the keep.

To the left was the entrance to the great hall where no doubt Conall and Uncle Torence were drinking ale by the fire, but instead, Cameron turned right and strode toward the steps that led up the nearest tower.

The tower where his cousin Cora, the now-widowed wife of Earl Seoras, had lived in a suite of second-story rooms that were empty after her recent departure from Campbell Castle.

Cameron's jaw tightened at the thought of how she had suffered during her marriage, but that was in the past, thankfully.

Cora hadn't tarried any longer than to give Cameron a tour of the living quarters in each of the four towers, and of all else that supported the household: the kitchens, the storerooms, the washrooms, on and on, until his head had pounded from the vastness of it. She hadn't said so, but he had sensed that she couldn't wait to leave behind what had been a deeply unhappy life, and a day later, she was gone.

A kiss upon his cheek and a wish for his health

and prosperity as baron of the fortress, and no mention at all, unlike so many others, about him finding a bride.

He had wondered as her small entourage had left the castle to return to her parents' home in north Argyll, if she might ever wed again after so unfortunate a first marriage—och, had he just heard a moan from the lass?

Cameron wasn't sure as he lunged up the tower steps to the second floor, her face still as pale as death. More bedchambers lay above on the third story, but this suite would be closer for Tobias, who did his best to keep up with him.

Another small moan—aye, this time he'd heard one indeed—made Cameron kick open the door to Cora's former rooms, startling a pair of maidservants with their feather dusters, who cried out in surprise.

"Fetch water! Clean cloths! A nightgown!" he shouted as he carried his still ominously limp load toward the huge four-poster bed, the wide-eyed women scurrying from the room. "Tobias, she might be waking—"

"Not waking, I fear," murmured the healer as he deposited the lantern on a table and rushed to Cameron's side, the young woman beginning to writhe in his arms. "She's delirious from the fever—aye, Laird, lay her down upon the bed."

Cameron did so even as a sharp elbow cuffed the side of his head, her arms and legs jerking and flailing.

"What else can I do? What else do you need?" He rubbed his ear and stepped aside as the healer began to rip away her clothing.

No difficult task, given their tattered condition, Tobias saying nothing but focusing intently upon his thrashing charge.

Her tunic gone, Cameron saw the binding wrapped around her upper body even as the healer tore at the soiled cloth with his beefy hands, easily freeing her from its bonds.

Her skin was bone white and creased with deep lines from so tight a constriction, her rose-hued nipples a stark contrast that made Cameron swallow hard.

Flattened nipples began to pucker and harden at the room's cool air, her full breasts taking their natural shape right before his eyes. Perfectly rounded... beautiful—

"Light a fire, Laird—aye, that's how you can help me."

Cameron swore under his breath, disgusted with himself for staring like an awestruck fool at the fever-stricken woman, even as she tossed like a wild thing upon the bed.

At once he did what Tobias had bidden him, bright flames soon crackling in the fireplace that had been heaped with logs in readiness for the suite's next inhabitant.

Not some important guest visiting the fortress, but a hapless released prisoner who began to sob in her delirium in so heart-wrenching a manner that Cameron's throat tightened.

He remained by the fire, for there was little else for him to do. A host of maidservants had rushed into the room, which had become a flurry of intense activity, Tobias directing them from the bedside.

Several assisted the healer in restraining the now naked young woman, while others quickly bathed and dried her and then dressed her in a linen nightgown, before tucking her beneath what appeared a mountain of blankets.

"Tae sweat away the fever," came Tobias's somber voice as if fully aware that Cameron watched silently from the fireplace. "At least we'll hope for as much..."

"Aye." Cameron said nothing else in response, for what more could he add? As the maidservants picked up the sodden cloths and towels from the floor, a stout pair still held down the young woman who bucked and tossed beneath the covers.

Meanwhile, Tobias busied himself with his potions and bottles, hastily concocting a dark syrupy brew that he poured into a wide spoon. "Tae make her sleep, Laird. It will be better this way."

Cameron could but nod, though he stepped closer to the bed when such an agonized cry tore from the woman's throat that the maidservants gasped.

"*Papa*, no! Noooooo!"

She thrashed so fiercely that those trying to hold her down struggled and cried out in dismay while Tobias rushed toward the bed.

"Laird, seize her by the shoulders—och, God!"

Before Cameron could reach her side, she sat bolt upright in her delirium and attempted to lunge from the bed—but he caught her before her bare feet touched the floor. Still she fought as if mustering every ounce of her strength, her eyes wide open now—and as vivid a blue as Cameron had ever seen.

"Papa! Stand up! Fight! Daran, help him—ah, God, they've struck you down, too. No, no, Finnegan, let me go. I must help them. *Help them*!"

Cameron tried to pin her forearms at her sides, but too late as she cuffed him with such force on the side of the head that he grimaced in pain. That brought an end to it, for with a resounding curse he sank onto the bed and hauled her into his arms, though she struggled mightily.

Weeping. Moaning. Shouting anew for her father... for Daran, whoever that man might be—och, what did it matter right now?

"Tobias, give her the damned potion," he shouted, which made Tobias rush forward with his spoon and thrust it into her mouth. Cameron could see that thankfully, much of the stuff was swallowed, though some trickled down her chin to drip onto her white nightgown.

"Give her another, man, for good measure," he ordered when still she thrashed against him, but already Tobias had refilled his spoon and once again, pushed the brew into her mouth.

The healer quickly forced several brimming spoonsful of water down her throat, too, which made her cough and sputter. Cameron feared for a moment she might choke, but then she slumped against him, her head lodged against his neck.

Her breathing hot and ragged upon his skin, her face wet, her chest heaving.

To his surprise, now that she was wedged within his embrace, he felt muscle in her upper arms where he had believed them thin and weak before.

No wonder she had struck him with such force, landing a blow that might rival a man's. He felt certain that she couldn't have been a prisoner for long to not have wasted away to mere skin and bone, as first feared.

Still holding her tightly, Cameron could feel her body growing limp and her breathing less labored, though her burning fever hadn't eased. He glanced at Tobias, who gestured for him to return her to the bed, which made him gather her against him and rise.

"She'll sleep into the night, Laird... if she survives that long. I'll send word tae you if anything changes—"

"No need, Tobias, I'm staying right here," Cameron cut him off as he settled her onto the mattress and covered her in blankets.

Her cheeks, flushed from her struggles and the heat consuming her body, were bright red against the stark white of the pillow. He pressed his palm to her forehead, wondering if he imagined that she didn't feel quite as warm as even moments before.

If she said anything further in her delirium, he

wanted to hear it—if only to give him some clue as to where in Ireland she might have come from.

A coastal town? When had she come to Scotland's shores? Why had she bound her breasts and dressed as a youth? Intuition told him some battle must have been fought where her father had fallen as well as the one she had called Daran. Were they dead? Alive? So many questions roiled within him even as she heaved a shuddering sigh and grew very still.

At once Cameron felt alarm and leaned over her, while Tobias rushed forward to press his fingers to her lips.

"No, Laird, she breathes... but barely. Nothing tae do now but wait, and pray. If you dinna mind, I'll go tend tae the other prisoner they found with her—"

"Aye, when he wakes, God willing, find out what you can and come at once tae tell me. If I have need of you, I'll send someone tae fetch you."

"As you wish, Laird. Keep her well covered and the fire stoked. Cool damp cloths upon her forehead might help."

Sighing, the healer left the bedside, while Cameron gestured for the maidservants still standing nearby to bring him a chair. He could have done so himself, but he didn't want to stray more than a footstep away from her on the chance that she might say something.

Anything. A whisper. A word.

Fresh questions seized him as he sat down heavily and stared at the young woman who slept now as if dead.

Her closely cropped hair framing a face that anyone would deem lovely now that the grime had been washed away—so how then could she have passed for a youth? A very pretty youth—och, that didn't even describe her.

The lass was beautiful. Her fine features perfectly proportioned, her skin as white as cream, her lips a soft red, though woefully chapped—yet with a fullness that made Cameron realize he was staring once again.

Aye, he had seen from where he stood by the fireplace as Tobias had stripped away the rest of her clothing that she was formed as beautifully. Long of limb, her waist narrow, her body lithe and not wasted away, either, as he had at first feared—

"By God, what goes on here?"

Conall's loud outburst jarring him, Cameron twisted around in the chair, scowling.

"Keep your voice down, will you? She's sleeping—"

"Aye, so Tobias told me as I passed him on the steps, yet it's *you* I'm surprised at, Cameron."

As Conall came around to the opposite side of the bed to stare down at the lass, he uttered a low whistle that grated upon Cameron even more.

"Dressed as a youth, was she? Here Uncle Torence and I were enjoying our ale by the fire with no clue as tae all the commotion, until I overheard some maidservants scurrying by. I came straightaway, thinking I'd find Tobias at her side—but not you, brother. And in Cora's rooms as well—"

"Where else was I tae take her?" Cameron cut him off, not liking at all Conall's evident appraisal of the lass. "The infirmary where she would lie on a cot surrounded by men?"

The harshness of his tone surprising even himself, Cameron turned back to the young woman even as Conall uttered another low whistle—and this time, his brother's gaze was squarely upon him.

"Ease yourself, Cameron. I can well understand that you consider the lass your responsibility given she's been suffering among us while we had no knowledge of it. I just know how you are when it comes tae women—and tae see you here sitting beside her..."

Conall grew silent, sighing, which made Cameron

grateful that his brother must have decided not to press him further, even as he met Conall's gaze.

"I'm hoping she'll reveal her name—or where she's come from. At least then if she doesn't survive, we might know how tae reach her family. Already she's cried out for her father and another man named Daran. A relative? A husband? You know many nobles in Éire have sided with King Robert because of his Irish wife. Mayhap the lass posed as a youth tae join her kinsmen—och, who can say? Pour some water into that basin, Conall, and bring it to me with some cloths."

"Oh, I'll fetch it for you, Laird," came an eager voice behind him, one of the maidservants still present rushing to oblige him.

Cameron didn't have to see the wench to know she was comely from the look upon Conall's face, his brother's appreciation of the fairer sex knowing no bounds.

As for him, Cameron gave the maidservant the barest of nods as she set the basin and linen cloths upon the bedside table, threw a bashful smile at Conall, and then scurried away to rejoin the other two by the door.

"Wait outside," he ordered gruffly. "If I need anything further, I'll call for you."

Cameron heard a murmuring of assent as all three maidservants left the room, and quickly, too, as if his tone had startled them. Meanwhile, Conall chuckled, though he sobered when the most plaintive sigh escaped the lass, making Cameron rise abruptly from the chair to lean over her.

Waiting. Wondering if she might say something from out of her deep sleep, but she did not.

Exhaling with frustration, Cameron soaked a cloth in the basin, wrung it out, and then folded it before placing the cool compress upon her forehead.

His hands looking so large and callused against the

smooth creaminess of her skin, his fingers lightly brushing her cheek.

A cheek that felt as soft as silk, making his breath catch—and Conall to utter another low whistle.

Cameron bristled. "*What?*"

"Nothing, brother, nothing. Since it appears you'll be occupied for a while, I'll let you know when your guests arrive—"

"No need. Send those women home, Conall."

"Aye, Laird Campbell, straightaway. Anything else?"

Cameron threw Conall a dark glance and shook his head, but his brother only grinned at him as he headed for the door.

A knowing grin, as if he had witnessed something that made him feel quite merry—och, Conall was simply thinking of that pretty maidservant waiting out in the hall.

Yet to be honest, Cameron considered as he focused once again upon the sleeping lass, he was surprised at himself, too.

He had never bestowed such attention upon a woman, *any* woman, but it was no hard task given her condition. She wasn't staring at him or trying to converse with him, his tongue feeling tight at the thought.

Giving terse orders to female servants didn't seem to trouble him, but engaging one-to-one with a woman was another thing entirely. He was grateful that he had only to sit there and hope she uttered something for him to latch onto so he could help her... whether she lived or died.

Aye, as Conall had said, the lass was *his* responsibility.

He was baron of Campbell Castle, and he wished now he hadn't banished the MacDougall guards and all the rest of their clansmen from the fortress, instead of imprisoning them after Earl Seoras had been slain. Already that act of mercy had come back to haunt him.

He would have strung them up by their thumbs to discover if any more such hellholes existed beneath the floor of the cells—

"Laird, the healer sent me tae fetch you tae the infirmary at once!"

Cameron lunged from the chair to glare at the red-faced manservant who had burst into the room, the older fellow breathing hard as if he had sprinted the entire way. "I told Tobias that I'd remain here and if he has news—"

"It's the prisoner found with the lass, Laird Campbell. He's awake—and he'll speak tae no one but you. Please, the healer said the man hasna long tae live!"

Cameron was already striding to the door, the servant stepping back with eyes wide as he passed by him.

"Are you coming, man?"

The maidservants standing in the hall gaped at him, too, and jumped when he shouted at them, "Tend tae the lass until I return. Go!"

They did, scrambling to oblige him even as Cameron set off at a run, the manservant hard upon his heels.

CHAPTER 3

"Does he live?" Cameron's roar echoed from the high ceiling of the infirmary, the healer rising from bending over a distant cot to beckon to him.

Cameron didn't look to the left or right at the men who had been Seoras's prisoners only days ago, some groaning in pain, but strode toward Tobias with his heart pounding. To his immense relief, he saw the healer's nod, though the man's expression was grave.

"He gave me his name, Laird, Finnegan—aye, and he's dying, barely able tae breathe. You must bend down if you're tae hear him..."

Tobias stepped aside for Cameron, who sank to his haunches beside the cot. The poor wretch already appeared more a white-faced corpse, Finnegan's cheeks ominously sunken beneath his sparse beard.

"You... you are the laird here?" came a rasping whisper, the man's bloodshot eyes drilling into Cameron's face.

"Aye, Cameron Campbell, baron of this fortress—"

"I told him that Earl Seoras was dead," Tobias broke in, leaning forward, "and that you've sworn allegiance tae King Robert—"

"Aye, King Robert..." echoed Finnegan weakly,

glancing from Tobias back to Cameron. "My mistress's relation—"

"Your mistress?"

Finnegan gave the barest nod, and grimaced as if the very motion of swallowing caused him great pain. "Not much time, Laird... forgive me. I'm dying, but if she still lives... then our efforts will not have been for naught. We gave her much of what little food they threw down to us... our water. The other men—the healer told me they're dead, God rest them forever. She will blame herself, I know it... my brave Aislinn..."

Cameron leaned closer as Finnegan grew still, closing his eyes, which made Cameron's heart pound again.

"The young woman with you. Her name is Aislinn?"

"Aye, Aislinn De Burgh. Her father, William, is our lord and leader... and cousin to King Robert's wife, Elizabeth. We came from Éire to fight for him... God help her, Aislinn stowed away on the ship. If I'd known, I would have stopped her... ah, please, water..."

Tobias immediately came forward and pressed a moist cloth to Finnegan's lips, which barely moved now, tears pooling in the corner of his eyes.

"Will she live, Laird Campbell?" came his plaintive query as he met Cameron's gaze. A bony hand, trembling, reached out to him, and Cameron clasped it. "Will she live?"

"The healer and I are doing what we can—everything we can for her," he murmured. "She called out for her father... and another man, Daran—"

"Her brother," Finnegan rasped. "Both taken prisoner... some of us, to this place... but them, we know not where. Lord De Burgh wounded and his son struck upon the head, so I fear—I fear—"

"Ease yourself, Finnegan," Cameron cut in quietly, the man clutching his hand with what must be the last remnant of his strength. Already Finnegan's grasp was weakening, his eyes starting to roll back into his head.

"Look after Aislinn, Laird Campbell... I beg you, and have patience. She's not like other women..."

Cameron didn't need Tobias to tell him that the man was breathing his last from the gurgling sound in his throat and the sudden limpness of his hand. Hoping that Finnegan could still hear him, he lowered his head to his ear.

"I will protect your mistress, Aislinn De Burgh, I swear it. Rest now, Finnegan, and go with God."

No answer came, and Cameron hadn't expected one. With the slightest last exhale of breath, the man was dead.

Sighing, Cameron drew up the sheet to cover Finnegan's face, and turned to Tobias. "My thanks for summoning me. At least now we know more about the lass—"

"A noble's daughter!" Tobias interjected, shaking his head as if he couldn't quite believe it. "Dressed like a lad, her hair cropped short like a lad's—och, and the men with her that died doing whatever they could tae help her survive. Their food, their water. A cousin of King Robert, no less, and a stowaway. What could it all mean?"

Grimly, Cameron shook his head as well and rose to stand over the cot. "See that Finnegan has a Christian burial—along with the others. If the lass survives, I'm certain she'll wish tae see where they've been laid tae rest."

"Aye, Laird."

Cameron didn't say anything further, his mind consumed by everything Finnegan had revealed as he strode back through the infirmary.

Aislinn De Burgh.

Aye, a noble name, a Norman name, her kinsmen no doubt of the lineage of knights and warriors who had conquered much of Ireland over a century ago. Yet to have come to Scotland to fight for King Robert... a treasonous act in the eyes of Edward, the English king.

A treasonous act most likely fueled by the fact that King Robert's wife had been taken prisoner a year past by that same ruthless king, determined to grind Scotland beneath the heel of his boot—aye, it was easy for Cameron to surmise as much.

His loyalty had been first and foremost to Gabriel MacLachlan, but they had fought for Earl Seoras MacDougall, their sworn overlord—though that allegiance had come to grate upon him as much as it had Gabriel.

Always a tyrant, Seoras had grown worse upon inheriting the earldom from his late father, his ruthless ambition to become king of Scots knowing no bounds.

Seoras had slain his own clansmen in his attempt to claim the throne. He had even ordered the murder of Gabriel's brother, Malcolm, and caused Gabriel to wed his lunatic sister, Magdalene MacDougall, in exchange for gold to help feed his starving people.

Cameron snorted, smiling wryly in spite of his dark mood, at the thought of the beauteous Mad Maggie who hadn't been a lunatic at all—and who had so completely won Gabriel's heart.

Aye, one could say that Cameron, Gabriel, Conall, and their kinsmen had committed treason as well, but Seoras—truly an evil man—had been put to the sword and tyranny overthrown. So Cameron could well understand what might have driven the De Burghs across the water to fight against their English sovereign in the name of their imprisoned cousin.

A father, William, a brother, Daran, and one long-limbed, red-haired young woman...

"Aislinn," Cameron said under his breath, testing the Irish name upon his tongue as a sudden commotion erupted at the entrance to the fortress.

Horses neighing.

Guards shouting to raise the massive iron gates.

The distant titter of female laughter. Had the prospective brides that his clan was trying to foist upon him arrived already?

His fists clenching, Cameron hoped that Conall had heard the commotion, too, and had left the training field to dispatch their unwelcome guests back to their homes—

"Och, Cameron, where are you going?" demanded Uncle Torence, who must have heard the ruckus outside from the great hall and rushed to the entranceway. "Will you not greet your honored guests?"

"No!" Cameron roared, his overriding thought to head back to Cora's suite of rooms—och, *Aislinn's* suite —and see how she fared.

Did she still sleep like the dead? Had her fever lessened? In truth, he didn't feel as pressing an urgency for her to say anything now, after what he learned from Finnegan, yet that didn't stop him from taking the tower steps three at a time.

He felt strangely breathless as he approached her door, and it wasn't because of exertion.

God help him, did she even still live? He was a warrior as accustomed to death as any other man who lived by the sword—so why was it suddenly so difficult for him to inhale?

He hesitated just outside the doorway, which was so unlike him as well, for a fighter who always charged headlong into battle.

Through the cracked door, he could hear the maidservants' anxious murmuring, which made his chest grow tight.

Aye, Aislinn must be dead, or else they wouldn't sound so nervous. Mayhap they feared finding him to give him the grim news?

Forcing himself to draw a steadying breath, Cameron pushed open the door that creaked on its hinges, causing the three maidservants to gasp and spin around from the bed.

~

Aislinn winced at the sudden creaking and tossed her head.

What was that grating sound? Like nails driving into her temples, she cried out and tried to open her eyes, but her eyelids felt leaden. All she could manage was a tiny slit, and she gazed uncomprehending at the trio of blurred figures standing over her—until panic filled her.

The Father, Son, and Holy Ghost—saints help her, she was dead and gone to heaven! No, no, she couldn't have died. How was she to find her father? Her brother? They needed her, *they needed her*!

Agony as gripping as the pounding pain in her head made her attempt to sit up, only to cry out again as feminine voices shrieked in surprise, and Aislinn fell back onto something plump and soft.

Her eyes half open now as another blurry shape came to tower over her—tall, forbidding, and with hair as black as night and a scowling countenance that made stark fear grip her.

No, no, no, it couldn't be! Not the Holy Trinity, but Satan himself staring down at her—ah, God, was she to be thrown into eternal hellfire?

Now Aislinn did try to fling herself as far away as she could from the dark apparition only to be thwarted by the heaviness covering her, making her feel as if she were drowning.

Drowning even as she heard a deep male voice commanding someone to fetch the healer, and then a frustrated shout. "By God, tell Tobias his blasted potion isna working!"

Tobias? Potion? Aislinn felt strong hands drawing her back and pressing her shoulders down, and now she screamed, as long and as loudly as she could muster as blackness enveloped her.

"No... no, *Papaaaaa*!"

~

"Go, I tell you. Run!"

Angered that the maidservants had gaped at him like frightened sheep before bobbing their heads and fleeing from the room, Cameron focused upon Aislinn, who had suddenly stopped fighting him and collapsed onto the mattress.

Her chest heaving beneath the nightgown.

Tears once more streaking her pale cheeks.

His ears ringing from the piercing screech that had burst from her and startled them all.

The maidservants jumping. Cameron cursing. What in God's name had frightened Aislinn so? All they were trying to do was help her. If not for all the blankets covering her, she might have thrown herself from the bed —and then what might have happened?

A broken arm or leg? A cracked skull? The only thing that gave Cameron some comfort after the wild frenzy he had just witnessed was that her fever seemed to have lessened.

He pressed his hand to her forehead to check again —aye, her skin was still warm but nothing like when he had left her earlier. So mayhap Tobias's potion was working after all, though for a few moments, Aislinn had managed to escape its effects and regained some of her senses.

What had she thought him, standing beside the bed and looking down at her? Any relief he had felt that she wasn't dead had fled at the look of sheer terror on her face, and then she had flung herself violently away from him.

Grateful again for the blankets that had prevented

her from tumbling to the floor, Cameron sighed heavily and sank into the chair still at the bedside.

For the first time in four days, he allowed the exhaustion that he'd held at bay to wash over him.

He had slept little since King Robert had bestowed Campbell Castle upon him, so many new and unfamiliar responsibilities for him to attend to. After this unexpected burst of strength from a young woman he had feared dead only moments ago, he felt as if he could close his eyes and join her in oblivion—aye, for indeed, once again, that same deep sleep had claimed her.

Lady De Burgh.

Unbidden, Finnegan's last words came back to him, making Cameron rub his temples in puzzlement.

Look after Aislinn, Laird Campbell... I beg you, and have patience. She's not like other women...

He had no idea what the Irishman could have meant —other than she possessed a ferocity of spirit that he had never before glimpsed in a woman.

To overcome the effects of a potion that thankfully appeared to be working? To try and fling herself with such force from the bed that Cameron had been hard-pressed to grab her back and hold her down?

She was stronger than he could ever have imagined, which wasn't at all like any noblewoman he'd ever encountered—not that there had been more than a few since he avoided women as best he could. Debora came to mind, Magdalene's older sister, who hadn't survived more than six months of marriage to a cruel husband. If any woman had embodied pure femininity, it had been her, though he had only observed her from afar.

Graceful, sweet-natured, soft-voiced, and as beautiful a countenance he had ever seen... until Aislinn. Yet such mildness of temperament had been her undoing, for she hadn't been able to withstand the brutality of a man who should have honored and cherished her.

Och, they had all been a wee bit in love with

Debora—he, Gabriel, and Conall when they were raw youths and served as guards at the fortress for Seoras's father, Earl Donal. Five years ago? Six? He was twenty-four now, those days so long ago...

Now Cameron did allow himself to close his eyes as a heaviness overwhelmed him—after a last glance at Aislinn, who slept deeply, if not peacefully.

Her eyelids had twitched as if she dreamed of something unpleasant, a low moan escaping her that made his throat tighten at all she had suffered.

Her father and brother wounded and taken prisoner and mayhap even executed by now, unless their captors were holding them for ransom. A common thing, if their nobility had been discovered before they were hanged or felt the descending blade of the executioner's axe.

The family separated, as Finnegan had said, the lass and her compatriots brought here and thrown into a pit, where she had been kept alive with offerings of their food and water. Their loyalty had astonished him, and made him wonder at what Finnegan had called her... *my brave Aislinn*.

Aye, there was still so much he didn't know, the unanswered questions preventing him from resting. Cameron opened his eyes to check on her, but nothing had changed. She slept while he could not, though his exhaustion felt bone deep.

Yet how was he going to discover more when she was fully conscious and looking him in the eye? Call for Conall to probe for answers while he stood mute at a distance, watching? His own tongue useless and grown thick from anxiety? How many times had he prayed for deliverance from this accursed affliction that had plagued him since boyhood?

Sighing with frustration, Cameron rose from the chair just as Tobias rushed into the room, with three serving maids right behind him.

"Laird, I've brought more potion!"

"Save it for when she wakes again, man," he said tightly, striding past the healer. "I need sleep. Dinna leave her side, do you hear me? I'll be back before it grows dark."

Cameron didn't wait for a reply, but left the room and tried to think only of his own bed on the second floor of the opposite tower.

A few hours' sleep, aye, that's all he would allow himself. Then he would return to Aislinn's side, where he intended to hold vigil the rest of the night.

As for when she opened her eyes—a vivid sky blue that had made him suck in his breath to see their beauty again—*och*!

He would cross that drawbridge when he came to it, God help him.

CHAPTER 4

"Cameron, *wake*. You must wake!"

Startled from a deep sleep, Cameron stared with some confusion at Conall, who shook him again.

Roughly.

"Brother, she's gone! The lass is gone."

Now Cameron sat upright, rubbing his face and then throwing aside the plain woolen blanket. He had not yet brought himself to sleep in the huge four-poster bed that had once belonged to Earl Seoras, choosing instead a simple cot like the men who now served under him, including Conall. He stared in disbelief at his brother, who nodded his head.

"Aye, gone like a puff of smoke and with no trace of her. I've ordered a search of the fortress and came tae wake you straightaway—och, it was one of the maidservants set tae watch her who came running tae find me. She said the lass jumped out of the bed and knocked poor Tobias tae the floor, walloped him on the head, and then ran from the bedchamber before they could stop her—"

"Tell me this is a dream, Conall—a blasted dream."

On her feet now, Cameron straightened his tunic twisted from sleep and grabbed the plaid breacan he had draped over a chair and wound it around himself and over one shoulder.

He had been so tired, he hadn't even kicked off his leather boots—a good thing given the need for haste. He retrieved his sword belt and fastened it around his waist while striding to the door, Conall just behind him, when a glance out the nearest window startled him—it was pitch dark.

"By God, what hour is it?"

"One or so before dawn. I came tae check on you after supper, but you were sleeping like the dead, Cameron. I didna see any reason tae wake you—och, until now, even though Uncle Torence wasna happy you didn't join us—"

"*Join you?*" Cameron whirled to face Conall, his brother's somewhat sheepish look making him bristle. "Dinna tell me..."

"Aye, another good reason not tae wake you, besides you getting so little rest these past days," Conall cut him off, holding out his upturned hands and shrugging. "It wasna my doing. I was all prepared tae send your unwanted guests home, but Uncle Torence insisted that they have supper and stay the night. The poor lasses were tired, Cameron, their horses needing rest, their entourage needing rest—"

"Not a dream, a damned nightmare," Cameron bit off, pushing past Conall, who once again came after him.

Aislinn gone.

Two clanswomen fancying themselves prospective brides under his roof.

"I suppose you kept them entertained," he muttered, not surprised that Conall heard him and gave a laugh.

"Aye, it wasna hard tae do. They're both comely enough, Cameron—one with hair the color of gold and the other a dark-haired beauty—och, but dinna fret. I kept my hands tae myself, though I canna say it was easy. After all, you dinna want a one of them, especially now that Aislinn De Burgh is here. Oh, aye, I saw how you looked at her, and it made my heart glad for you—"

"Conall, *enough!*" Once again, Cameron had stopped to round on his brother, but Conall skirted him and hastened down the hall toward the tower steps.

"I'll go check on the search. Where shall I meet you?"

"The great hall at first light. I want tae speak with Tobias first and mayhap search the tower."

Conall waved his hand in assent and sprinted down the steps, Cameron not far behind.

His brother's athletic prowess had always astonished him, Conall able to outrun most men, outwrestle them, out-throw them, truly any sort of contest that required strength, agility, or fleetness of foot. And for a man nearly as tall as him and as well-muscled—och, no wonder women couldn't resist him.

At the bottom of the steps, Cameron did his best to thrust away any thought of the Campbell lasses who'd come to meet him, and focused only upon Aislinn. He could hear Conall, already disappeared outside, roaring to the men searching for her if she'd been found—but no hue and cry came after, which made Cameron's heart start to pound.

Where the devil could she have gone? Surely if she had run from the tower and out into the bailey, someone would have seen her. No doubt looking like a ghost in that white nightgown and with that startling shock of red hair.

Mayhap she hadn't come down the steps at all, but was hiding in some room not far from her bedchamber —aye, he could hope. She wasn't well. She would catch her death from a chill or flare her fever red-hot again.

It seemed a moment more and Cameron had lunged up the opposite tower and burst into Aislinn's room, only to see the teary-eyed maidservants huddled around Tobias, who sat in a chair, holding his head.

"Good God, man, are you bleeding?"

Tobias nodded, a cut above his right temple that one of the serving maids was blotting with a wadded cloth. At once Cameron saw the brass candlestick that had rested upon the bedside table now on the floor, the wax candle broken in two as if someone had trod upon it.

Aislinn's weapon, and wielded so skillfully that Tobias, no matter a brawny fellow, hadn't known what hit him.

Cameron glanced around the room for whatever else she might have grabbed on her way out the door. Och, one of a pair of taller and heavier candlesticks from the carved mantelpiece above the fireplace was gone; he had noted them the day before when stoking the fire.

"Did she say anything?" he queried, focusing back on the healer.

"She screamed like an Irish banshee!" came Tobias's affronted response, though he winced at once from the pain it cost him. "Screamed and knocked me down and then struck me so hard I feared she cracked my skull. I had the spoon almost tae her mouth when she awoke of a sudden and gaped at me as if I was trying tae poison her. Hoyden! Fiend!"

Tobias looked so outraged, so affronted, mayhap his masculine pride bruised as well to have been bested by a woman, that Cameron felt the strangest urge to chuckle. Yet he kept his expression somber as one of the maidservants broke into sobs and crossed herself.

"It was a terrible thing tae see, Laird—terrible. Her eyes so wild. Her nightgown whirling around her. We feared for our lives, we did!"

"Did you see which way she ran? Down the hallway toward the steps?"

Now all three women looked at him blankly, Cameron deciding not to waste any more time with questions. Instead he strode to the door, a serving maid crying after him.

"She grabbed another candlestick, Laird. Like a sword she carried it, I've never before seen the like. Take care when you find her that she doesna strike you as well!"

Considering that very thought himself, Cameron glanced down the hallway toward the steps, but his instincts told him that she hadn't run that way. But where...?

A low creak made Cameron look to the left, his gut clenching at the cracked door that led to a smaller, winding staircase.

Cora had shown it to him, a more private way to venture to the tower's upper floors, not that Cameron had thought he would have need of it. Yet what if Aislinn had ducked in there thinking it would lead down— when it only went up?

His hand on the hilt of his sword—God help him, not to strike her but to parry a blow if need be—and holding his breath, Cameron cautiously opened the door only to hear a vexing creak that made him clench his teeth.

Good God, did all the door hinges in this place need oil? He saw, too, that the stairway was as black as pitch, no wall sconces lit, which was something else that must be remedied. Otherwise, how was one to safely navigate the stone steps?

Cameron did fully draw his sword now and left the door wide open for the light from the hall, where at least candles sputtered. He ducked his head beneath the low entrance and proceeded to climb the steps, his eyes quickly adjusting to the darkness even as he scanned ahead for any sight of a white nightgown.

His heartbeat seemed to pound in his ears over the

stillness in the musty-smelling stairway, his careful foot-falls the only other sound.

No screeches or wild outcries from a surprise at-tacker wielding a candlestick, which made him realize as he climbed upward, Aislinn wasn't hiding in the stairway—at least not between the second and third floor.

Would she have ventured further to the last floor, or gone out the door he searched for now? His gut in-stincts told him the latter, for no doubt she had seized upon the quickest escape she could find.

With light no longer filtering from below, he'd climbed too high in the tower, Cameron had to grope in the blackness for the door latch. He would search this floor first and if he didn't find her, he would make his way at once to the next. He had told Conall he would meet him at first light, and time was quickly passing.

Cameron pushed open the door; thankfully, no jar-ring creak heralded his presence. He stepped out into the hall and paused for a few moments to listen, but he heard nothing other than the whistling wind beyond the tower's walls.

He hadn't noticed it before, so that told him mayhap an early morning storm was brewing. A good thing, the land needed more rain, but right now he needed quiet so he might hear—

"Och, will it be that simple?" Cameron said to him-self at the piteous sound of weeping coming from fur-ther down the hall. No one occupied this floor right now, no reason for any servants to be up here before dawn, so it had to be Aislinn.

He lowered his sword, not willing yet to sheathe it on the chance that a candlestick might come flying to-ward him—and walked as silently as he could until he reached the bedchamber that Magdalene and Gabriel had occupied a few days past.

A bedchamber where her lunatic mother had been

imprisoned and died—och, Seoras had shown his cruelty once again to lodge them where the poor woman had so grievously suffered. Aislinn's weeping had lessened, and instead Cameron heard sniffles until he took another step and a floorboard creaked—the devil take it, *more* repairs to be made?

He didn't make another move, the sound of footfalls running across the floor inside the bedchamber making him grow tense to his boots.

Was she waiting with her candlestick raised to knock him on the head when he pushed open the door? Was she hiding instead, mayhap hoping against hope that whoever had strayed to this floor would simply go away?

Cameron waited another moment, preparing to kick open the door so violently that she might drop her weapon—och, the last thing he wanted was to suffer a blow like Tobias. Yet what harm might such a forceful entry do when his aim was for Aislinn to trust him? To understand that he only wished to help her?

Sighing heavily, Cameron sheathed his sword and took a step toward the door... until it occurred to him that within a moment he would meet her face-to-face.

Stare into her stunning eyes.

Speak to her. Already he felt a fine sheen of sweat around the collar of his tunic, his palms growing damp, too.

Why was he so afflicted... *why*? How could a warrior triumphant in so many battles feel nearly unmanned at the thought of conversing with so beautiful a woman?

Despair filling him, Cameron considered leaving her to hide in the bedchamber until he could summon Conall—but the door flew open and slammed against the inner wall so suddenly that he sucked in his breath in surprise.

He had no more than an instant to blink and she was upon him in a swirl of white nightgown and long limbs. The candlestick raised high and what he swore was a battle cry bursting from her throat.

Somehow he dodged her weapon, but not fast enough to prevent the metallic edge of the candlestick from grazing his head, the sharp, stinging sensation making Cameron roar in fury.

"Woman!"

Aye, conversing was one thing, but facing an opponent determined to strike him down was entirely another. Cameron grabbed a slim arm and wrested the candlestick from her. Yet if he had thought that might end her attack, he was wrong, when she grabbed the hilt of his sword and drew it so swiftly from his belt that he stared at her in utter disbelief.

Never before in his life had that happened— Cameron so stunned that he nearly lacked the presence of mind to jump back when she swung at him as ably as any swordsman he'd ever seen.

Her eyes locked with his in the heat of combat.

Her bare feet set wide and planted firmly on the floor as she stood tall and swung again, this time barely missing his abdomen as he jumped back a second time.

Her expression not like anything he had seen before on a woman, implacable and fiercely determined as she lifted the sword high and swung again—Cameron awestruck now as he dodged death a third time.

As if an apparition from centuries past, he could not take his eyes from her and he didn't dare. He had heard tales of Viking shield-maidens that fought side by side with men, his own ancestors of Norse blood. She raised the sword again, yet Cameron could see from the shakiness of her grasp that she had tired, her breathing harsh and ragged.

Still she came toward him while he took another step back, and no matter how magnificent she appeared, he'd had enough of his sword being used against him.

He waited for the right instant with the blade descending toward his shoulder, dodged and then pivoted to grab the hilt from her hand—just as he heard Conall's voice down the hall.

"By God, brother, I thought she was going tae kill you!"

Cameron didn't answer, his own breathing harsh to his ears as he levelled the sword at the base of her throat to dissuade her from making another move.

Still an opponent to him in his mind, for no matter her evident exhaustion, her tightly balled fists told him that she hadn't given up on fighting.

Her gaze, darkened to a turbulent blue, fixed upon him.

"Lady De Burgh, no matter what you must think, you've no enemies here. We're all loyal tae King Robert. Earl Seoras, the bastard who imprisoned you, is dead and Clan MacDougall defeated. I'm the laird now, Baron Cameron Campbell, and I swore tae Finnegan, just before he died, that I would protect you—"

"Finnegan is dead?"

Her stricken voice as light as a whisper, Cameron saw her falter as Conall came up behind him, his brother's whoop of astonishment ringing around them.

"Did you hear yourself, Cameron? I'd swear you're cured—och, *catch her!*"

Cameron already had, one arm flying around her waist to prevent her from collapsing to the floor even as he sheathed his sword.

An instant more and he'd swept her up to carry her down the hall, her face stark white as Conall strode alongside him.

"You're bleeding, Cameron."

"Aye."

"Your own sword?"

"Candlestick."

Conall's low whistle grating upon him, Cameron

said nothing more, Aislinn De Burgh once more limp in his arms.

His heart thundering at how much he had said to her, his own astonishment at himself tenfold that of Conall's.

Yet Cameron wasn't cured, sweat dripping from his brow and causing his flesh wound to burn, which made him curse vehemently.

At once he saw her flinch, so she hadn't fainted, but mayhap was overcome by shock. Clearly she cared for Finnegan, and coupled with exhaustion from attacking him, the grim news had proved too much for her.

One good sign, though, her fever was gone. He could feel the normal warmth of her body through her nightgown, Cameron dropping his gaze to the steady rise and fall of her breasts.

Her taut nipples pressed against the thin fabric made his throat grow tight, an arresting sight he'd noticed moments ago when she had been swinging at him with his sword.

His sword.

The tempting pucker of those nipples could have gotten him killed—and now he nearly stumbled at the bottom of the tower steps if Conall hadn't grabbed his elbow to steady him.

"Easy, brother, you dinna want tae drop her."

"Aye, if you're going to drop me, I'll walk on my own," came an indignant sputter as Aislinn stared up at him, her cheeks grown bright pink. "*Protect me*, will you? Then I'll ask you to stop ogling me as if you've never seen a woman's breasts before, Laird Campbell. Let me down!"

CHAPTER 5

Aislinn didn't know if Cameron looked more stunned that she had recovered herself or at what she had just said—but her feet touched the stone floor so abruptly that she gasped.

He might have well as dropped her, for she faltered again, her knees as shaky as moments ago when she'd heard about Finnegan's death.

Ah, God, the man had been like a father to her. Blinking back tears, she told herself fiercely to keep her wits about her as she stared from one strapping Scotsman to the other, both men gaping at her.

Both men as black-haired and handsome as any she had ever seen, with eyes as deep blue as the Irish Sea. Cameron stood a wee bit taller than the other one, who must be a younger brother for how closely they resembled each other.

As if reading her mind, he stepped forward and offered a gallant bow, a grin splitting his face when he straightened.

"Conall Campbell, beautiful lady, and I'm glad tae see that you're looking so much better."

Beautiful lady? At once Aislinn deemed him for what Conall must be, a flatterer and seducer of women, how-

43

ever good-natured—aye, and she intended to stay far away from him.

As for his towering older brother, she had never seen a man look more ill at ease, his expression strained and a fine sheen of sweat upon his brow.

So different from the fearsome warrior Cameron had appeared when he had seized his sword from her— aye, that would never have happened if she hadn't been weakened by imprisonment.

Gritting her teeth against the lightheadedness that threatened once again to overwhelm her, Aislinn shot a glance around her to see that the three of them weren't alone.

Wide-eyed servants, men and women alike, stood outside a cavernous great hall, while guards clustered near an arched doorway that must lead outside. All of them stock-still and silently watching as if uncertain what to do.

Yet Aislinn knew exactly what she needed to do. She looked down at the linen nightgown that did little to hide her nakedness, and then back to Cameron.

"Laird Campbell, I want my clothes... my tunic and trousers."

No sooner had she uttered the words than a deafening crack of thunder seemed to make the walls shake and the servants gasp, while Conall gave a quick glance at Cameron, who appeared even more uncomfortable than before.

"They've been discarded," came Conall's reply as if speaking for his brother. "Probably burned by now. Our healer, Tobias—the unfortunate fellow you cracked on the head with a candlestick—had tae rip them off you when you were delirious with fever. I dinna imagine you recall any of that—"

"Saints help me, I thought it was a terrible dream," Aislinn said more to herself, finding it most strange for Cameron not to have answered her demand himself.

Everything around her seemed a mixed-up dream, bits and pieces tumbling through her mind.

Aye, vaguely she remembered fighting and flailing and tasting something syrupy and most foul until blackness had claimed her.

Then what she'd been certain was a worse nightmare, Satan leaning over her... an apparition that she could see now had looked decidedly like Cameron Campbell.

Then more recently when she had awoken with a start, and feared that the burly fellow trying to stick a spoon into her mouth was an enemy, her one thought had been to strike him down and escape from the room.

Yet the stairway she'd found had only gone upward, leaving her disoriented and desperately searching for a place to hide until she could decide upon her next move.

Only then had she surrendered to tears of frustration and confusion—aye, useless tears—until she'd heard a creaking floorboard...

"You're shivering, Lady De Burgh," Conall's voice broke into her racing thoughts. "If you'd allow me tae escort you back tae your rooms—a fine suite where I'm sure you'll be comfortable. Then we'll find you some clothing, though you see we're not much for trousers here—"

"Aye, you Highlanders are a strange lot," Aislinn cut him off, glancing at their bare knees and thickly muscled calves. "Running around bare-arsed beneath your tunics—and don't think to bring me a woman's gown for I'll not wear it!"

She took a few steps backward as her stomach growled loudly, Aislinn feeling so famished of a sudden that she feared she might faint.

"By God, fetch the woman some food. Some water!" came Cameron's roar at the servants standing nearby, while Conall caught her forearm as if to steady her though Aislinn tried at once to wrench herself free.

"Have you not done enough fighting for one day?" he reprimanded her in a low voice while glancing at Cameron, who had stridden off toward the great hall. "You nearly skewered my brother with his own sword when he's done nothing but try tae help you since you were pulled out of that hole. Now come or I swear I'll pick you up and carry you—"

"I can walk," she retorted, though in truth her knees felt wobbly, Conall not letting go of her arm as he followed after Cameron.

The servants had scattered and the guards were gone as if his thunderous command had snapped them out of some trance, while the place had erupted into a flurry of activity.

Wall torches lit to brighten the high-ceilinged space, while she could see Cameron himself stoking the flames in a massive fireplace, his broad back to her and Conall as they drew closer.

Long trestle tables were already set for the morning meal, which made Aislinn wonder when more occupants of the fortress would flood into the hall to eat, her stomach growling even more loudly.

Conall hadn't said another word to her, any congeniality she had felt from him having disappeared as his gaze seemed to be focused upon Cameron.

"Do you always speak for your brother?" she demanded as Conall steered her toward a table near the warming fire. "Who is the true laird here? *You* or him—oh!"

He had stopped so abruptly that Aislinn stumbled, but his tight grip upon her arm kept her from falling. Yet if he'd meant to say something, another terse command from Cameron, his back still turned to them, made Conall once again propel her forward.

"Tell her tae sit down."

"My brother wants you tae sit down—"

"I heard him!" Aislinn protested as she was led to a carved chair, clearly one of honor, as most of the other seating in the hall was comprised of rough-hewn benches. The furnishings reminded her so much of her father's hall in Wexford, but she had no more time to think upon it as she was unceremoniously pushed down into the chair, Conall finally releasing her.

She rubbed her forearm, glowering at him as he frowned back at her, the amiable younger brother replaced by a grim-looking warrior who struck Aislinn as somehow overly protective of Cameron—though she couldn't imagine why.

She had seen few Highlanders as formidable-looking as Laird Campbell, even with his back still to them as he appeared to stare into the fire.

His midnight hair skimmed immense shoulders that looked as powerful as his muscular arms as he prodded and poked at the crackling logs, though the blazing fire was more than stoked by now.

Whatever was he doing? Some instinct told her that mayhap he was lost in thought, or even trying to distract himself, until another roared command split the air and made Aislinn jump in her chair.

"*Blast and damn, where is the food?*"

As if his demand caused the double doors at one end of the hall to fly open, servants came running with pitchers and steaming bowls and trenchers laden with what Aislinn could smell was freshly baked bread—making her mouth water.

It seemed another moment and she had a steaming portion of porridge set in front of her, another servant pouring a generous amount of cream onto the top. She was so hungry that she couldn't wait any longer, and grabbed a thick slice of bread slathered with golden butter from a trencher and thrust it into her mouth.

"Tell her tae eat more slowly or she'll choke—as well as make herself sick."

"Aye, you'd best eat slowly or you'll choke," came Conall's response, which made Aislinn bristle.

She wanted to shout at him that she'd heard Cameron—aye, she didn't need Conall to repeat everything the man said—though her mouth was too full to speak.

The bread tasted like heaven—aye, the butter both sweet and salty on her tongue as she chewed and chewed, her cheeks puffed out like a squirrel's.

Finally she was able to swallow, but just as Cameron had said, she began to cough and wheeze as the bread clogged her throat. Aislinn grabbed for a cup that had been filled to the brim with water. She was so desperate to drink that she spilled much of the contents down the front of her nightgown, but she didn't care—saints help her, she *was* choking!

"Dinna stand there, Conall, pound her on the back."

As if he intended for her to struggle for a heart-stopping moment, Conall moved slowly to her side and gave her a sharp thump in the middle of her spine.

She had just taken another desperate swallow of water, the liquid spewing out of her mouth even as she swallowed the lump of bread, Conall gazing at her wryly.

"You see? My brother said tae—"

"I know! Eat slowly or I'll choke," Aislinn cut him off. She felt so foolish sitting there in her water-splattered nightgown, while Conall sat down opposite her and calmly dug a spoon into his bowl of porridge.

She glanced at Cameron and caught him looking at her out of the corner of his eye—but he turned back to the fire almost at once and left her wondering again whatever was the matter with the man.

She could sense from the tension in his broad shoulders that his unease had only mounted, the sweat upon his face glistening in the firelight. Conall glanced at him, too, his expression almost resigned as he focused once more on his porridge, while Aislinn sampled some from her bowl.

Like the bread, she took far too big a mouthful, but as she focused as well on the food in front of her and ate her fill, the terrible pains in her stomach began to ease.

Pains she'd suffered for long days in that stinking black hole where she and Finnegan and three of her father's men had been imprisoned, Aislinn certain as time wore on that they were all going to die.

A pang of guilt ripped through her that she hadn't asked about the others, but something told her that the news would be the same.

Finnegan, the other three. All dead, or surely she would have been told otherwise.

It seemed an uprising had occurred while she and her clansmen had suffered in that prison, for the Mac-Dougall guards had jeered at them quite plainly that the fortress was the domain of Earl Seoras.

She had never seen him, but it had been his orders that they be thrown into the fetid hole to rot—aye, so the guards had taunted them.

"Filthy Irishmen! Earl Seoras despises your kind. This will teach you for crossing the water tae fight for Robert the Bruce—the traitorous usurper!"

Thank God they had not discerned she was a woman, Finnegan warning her all along when they had dropped their weapons and been taken prisoner not to utter a word for fear that the timbre of her voice would give her away. He had told her that male garb and bound breasts would not be enough to save her even if she spoke in guttural tones, and she had heeded his advice—ah, Finnegan, God rest you.

Aislinn shoved away the bowl, overcome by fresh guilt at how much she had eaten when she and her clansmen had been given so little food... tainted, foul-tasting water and moldy bread.

To a man, they had refused to eat or drink at all if she didn't take some of their ration, tears filling her eyes at their selfless sacrifice. Dead, all dead—

"Now that she's eaten, Conall, ask her what happened tae her father, William De Burgh, and the other one she cried out for, Daran—"

"I can hear you, Laird Campbell," Aislinn burst out in frustration, swiping away the tears that had trickled down her face. "Why will you not speak to me yourself like you did in the tower? Do you not think it strange at all, asking your brother to repeat everything you say? If you want answers to your questions, then face me like the baron you say you are and ask them. I'll not speak another word otherwise, I vow it!"

Her strident words ringing around them, Aislinn saw that Conall had dropped his spoon into his bowl and looked at his brother, who hadn't moved an inch from staring into the fire.

Servants stood wide-eyed, too, she imagined because she had spoken so defiantly to their laird, until they began to back away as if expecting some explosion from him at any moment.

Yet no explosion came, though Aislinn noticed, too, that Cameron's hand had tightened into a fist around the poker as he slowly turned to face her.

His dark scowl made her heartbeat quicken, and she felt a stab of regret that she had lashed out at him.

If what Conall had said was true, and Cameron had been doing his best to help her, then the least she could do was act civilly toward him.

She twisted further in her chair to face him, and at once saw his gaze drop to the bodice of her nightgown, which clung to her skin for the water she'd spilled upon herself.

The curved outline of her breasts and rosy shade of

her nipples visible beneath the sodden fabric. She had been so ravenous that she hadn't noticed, but now her face grew warm at the intensity with which he stared at her.

Still he said not a word, but instead set down the poker and unwound his breacan and tossed it at her. A full stomach having sharpened her reflexes, she caught the garment and draped it over her shoulders to cover herself, imagining that was exactly what he had intended for her to do.

Still he was silent, a raw tension in his face that made her wonder anew what plagued him even as she noted the breacan bore a decided masculine scent.

Wood smoke. Sweat. And something else she couldn't name... and which she realized must be of the very man himself, her cheeks flaring again.

Not because she didn't like it, but because she did.

"*Speak*, Lady De Burgh."

CHAPTER 6

At Cameron's terse command, Aislinn heard a sharp intake of breath from Conall. Yet she didn't spare him a glance even as she felt some astonishment that he hadn't focused once upon her damp bodice.

Not because she had wanted him to, but because it wasn't like a seducer at all—saints help her, what sort of men were these Campbells?

One a bold flatterer and the other, as reluctant as a monk who had taken a vow of silence to utter more than a couple brusque words!

"My father and brother were taken prisoner by English soldiers—along with the few men that weren't slaughtered. They were attacked the moment they set foot upon the shore, as if lookouts had been posted to watch for them—an ambush!"

"*English*, you say?"

Aislinn saw that Cameron's shoulders had tightened, his blue eyes boring into her.

"Aye, and Scotsmen among them—the traitors. All had been arranged, my father believing he'd be met by some of King Robert's forces, but he was betrayed! Everything happened so fast—ah, God."

Now Aislinn swallowed hard as her throat constricted at the terrible memories that assailed her.

"My clansmen were cut down right and left as they fought alongside my father and Daran, who were struck down, too. Finnegan and I and three others had been the last to disembark from the ship and were wading ashore—Laird Campbell, do they live? My kinsmen?"

A grim shake of his head made Aislinn feel sick inside, the food she'd eaten suddenly roiling in her stomach. It was hard to continue, but somehow she did. "The English took my father and brother... and the Scotsmen brought us here—"

"How long ago?" Conall had blurted out this query, and then glanced at his brother, who still had his gaze fixed upon Aislinn.

"Aye, how long?"

Cameron's voice had sunk to a harsh whisper, which made her shake her head.

"I-I cannot say. We were shoved into that pit, no light at all to tell night from day. Finnegan managed to count eleven days, mayhap twelve... but by then we'd all grown so weak. We never knew when they would bring us food and water, so there was no way for us to know how much time had passed—"

"Nearly two weeks, then," Conall broke in again, Cameron nodding grimly.

"Anything beyond that and they would have all been dead," he said more to Conall, no longer looking at her. "Finnegan told me that she stowed away on her father's ship. I canna believe when the battle erupted that Lord De Burgh was pleased tae see her—"

"Aye, I stowed away because I wanted to fight for King Robert as much as my father and Daran. I would have challenged those accursed English, too, if Finnegan hadn't held me back!"

Outraged that they were speaking about her as if she wasn't there, Aislinn rose from her chair so abruptly that it crashed to the floor.

"You saw yourself, Laird Campbell, that I can wield

a sword as well as any man. Finnegan taught me to defend myself and this would have been my chance to prove to my father that I can fight, too. Yet the battle was over before it had even begun and Finnegan held me back! He was my teacher, aye, a second father to me, but for that I'll never forgive him—"

"He saved your life, woman!"

Aislinn gaped at Cameron, who had taken several steps toward her and reached out as if he wanted to shake her, though instead he gestured at Conall.

"Get her out of my sight, now! I swore tae protect her, aye, but it's more likely I'll be forced tae protect the lass from herself."

Conall lunged around the table and caught Aislinn before she could dodge him, but not fast enough to prevent her from grabbing a bread knife from the table. Within an instant, the blade was pressed to Conall's throat, his eyes widening in disbelief.

"Uh... Cameron—"

"I don't need or want your protection, Laird Campbell," Aislinn said tightly, surprised herself at her drastic action as Cameron's countenance growing truly thunderous. "I want you to swear to me now in front of Conall and everyone else in this hall that you'll take me to King Robert. Not tomorrow or a week from now —*we leave this morning*! He'll know how to find my father and brother. We're his wife's cousins after all. He'll be honor bound to help me—"

"They're dead by now, nothing tae find," came Cameron's grim response, Aislinn aware that he had edged closer as she shook her head at him.

"No. The English had to have known my father is a nobleman and seized him for ransom! Word has surely flown to Wexford and gold is being gathered—"

"Aye, and once delivered tae his captors, they'll be executed all the same."

"No, I don't believe you! Now swear or you'll have

your brother's death on your hands." Aislinn stood her ground as Cameron stepped closer, which forced her to press the blade harder against Conall's throat. She hadn't meant to pierce him, but the tip of the knife broke his skin, a trickle of blood oozing forth.

"Cameron... by God, *swear tae the lass*, will you?"

Her heartbeat thundering at Conall's hoarse plea, Aislinn wondered with mounting dread if Cameron would lunge at her even as he glanced beyond them to a commotion at the entrance to the hall.

"Aye, I swear it."

"Say it again," she demanded, "and louder for all to hear."

"*I swear it!*"

Now Cameron looked truly furious as Aislinn dropped the knife to the floor, Conall rubbing his throat and starting to chuckle.

"A brilliant move for getting your way, Lady De Burgh—"

"Aislinn," she cut him off, retreating a few steps backward as a buzz of voices grew louder, though she didn't dare to turn around to look. "No one at home calls me Lady."

"Aye, with you in your man's garb, I can see how that might cause some confusion," Conall countered with amazing good spirits considering she had just held a knife to his throat and drawn blood. He seemed about to say more, but a feminine squeal across the hall made them both turn around.

"Oh, Laird Campbell, is it really you?"

Aislinn watched in wonderment as a young woman with flowing blond hair hastened toward them in a flutter of green silk... while on her heels came another one, dark-haired and a wee bit on the plump side in a purple gown embroidered with gold.

Their faces alight with smiles that soon turned to looks of dismay as a gruff curse behind her made her whirl around to see Cameron striding away—the whole while barking orders at Conall as servants scattered to get out of his path.

"Take Aislinn back tae her room."

"Aye, brother."

"Then send those women home!"

"Aye, straightaway—but might they have breakfast first?"

Cameron didn't answer, Aislinn wholly astonished as he slammed open the double doors that must lead to the fortress kitchens and disappeared.

Both she and Conall accosted in the next moment by the two women who not only looked crestfallen, but had burst into tears.

"Conall, where has he gone?" cried the blonde, while the dark-haired one set off as if to follow after Cameron, though Conall quickly caught her by the elbow and steered her back.

Meanwhile, Aislinn had begun to cough at the overpowering scent of roses emanating from them, her eyes watering.

"Did you douse yourselves with an entire vial of perfume?" she demanded, not surprised that the young women both looked her up and down, still teary-eyed and hiccoughing. "That alone would send any man running. Saints above, do you blame him?"

The two blinked at Aislinn as if they hadn't fully comprehended what she'd said, but a scarce moment more and they both broke out in fresh wails, now clinging to each other.

"Och, God help me," Aislinn heard Conall mutter, though an instant later he bestowed the most handsome smile upon the women, which made their weeping cease almost at once.

As Aislinn watched in sheer amazement, he took them both by the arm and led them to the table, his soothing tone as smooth as satin.

"Ease yourselves, lasses. I know how much you'd like tae meet Cameron, but he has tae leave this very morning—"

"*Leave?*" blurted the blonde, glancing toward the doors where Cameron had disappeared.

"Aye, important business with King Robert. So you'll have tae leave us as well and return tae your homes—but mayhap you'll meet my brother another time. Now, why dinna you enjoy some porridge and cream while I attend tae our other guest—"

"Does she hope as well tae become Laird Campbell's bride?" The dark-haired one looked quite doubtful as her gaze again swept Aislinn from head to foot—which made her bristle.

"*Bride*? Me? You can have him with all of his scowls and little to say!" With that, she drew Cameron's breacan more tightly around her shoulders and left Conall staring after her as she proceeded across the hall, though he caught up with her before she'd gone halfway, and took her arm.

"My brother's orders," he began, but she yanked herself away.

"You don't have to accompany me, I can find my own way," she insisted, giving a nod back to the table where he had left the two women. "Prospective brides? Laird Campbell doesn't look to me like he's eager to marry—disappearing from the hall like he did. What ever is the matter with him? You'd think he was afraid of women the way he went running—"

"Not afraid, just afflicted—och, he wouldna be pleased if I told you."

Conall looking suddenly as somber as when she'd held the knife to his throat, Aislinn had no desire to prod him.

No matter what plagued Cameron, she needed him to escort her to King Robert—for how else would she have a hope of finding her father and Daran? The masculine smell of the breacan a relief to her after that cloud of perfume, she found herself nonetheless pricked by curiosity.

Afflicted? By what?

As if reading her mind, Conall gave a low chuckle, which made her cheeks begin to burn.

"What? If you're going to tell me, then go on with it! It probably would be a good thing to know since we'll be traveling together—"

"Shyness, the crippling kind. A fearsome warrior in battle, but when facing a woman—or God help him, having tae speak tae one..." Conall fell silent and shrugged as he walked up the tower steps beside her, while Aislinn was certain she had never felt her heart beating faster.

Shyness? Cameron Campbell? A laird and baron? This revelation was so incongruous to what she'd seen of the man, his every move bespeaking strength and power.

Yet what of his few words? His hesitancy to speak to her? Cameron staring for so long into the fire as if he couldn't bring himself to look at her—

"Dinna tell him that I told you, for he'll never forgive me." Conall's voice broke into her thoughts, the two of them already to her door before she had even realized it. He faced her, still looking so serious, until the slightest smile touched his lips. "Though mayhap that wouldna be such a bad thing, for him tae know. I've never seen him take such care of anyone, sitting beside your bed, hoping you might say something in your fever that might help him find your kinsmen—"

"He did that for me?" Suddenly breathless, though she didn't know why, Aislinn felt a strange warmth when Conall nodded.

"I couldna believe my eyes, but there he was, laying a cool cloth on your forehead. He carried you himself tae this room, and helped the healer—"

"Rip away my clothes?" Aislinn clutched the breacan as Conall shook his head.

"I dinna know, but what matter? Cameron helped you—and the moment he heard you'd gone missing, his only thought was tae find you. I still canna believe you attacked him with his own sword—och, woman, but he spoke tae you unlike I've ever heard him before. And then in the hall, moments ago? Aye, only a few words, but he looked at you all the while—and I've *never* seen him do that before. Mayhap you're the cure he's been praying for..."

Conall's last words spoken more to himself than her, Aislinn didn't know why he'd shared so much with her or why her heart raced all the faster.

All she knew was that she wanted to disappear into her room to gather her wits about her and to catch her breath. She spun around and fumbled with the latch until Conall reached around her and pushed open the door for her. She ducked inside, and would have closed the door on him if he hadn't stuck his boot against the jamb to stop her.

She stared at him in surprise, wondering what he had in mind, but she saw no flatterer or seducer of women there—only what she sensed was a man concerned for his elder brother.

"Are you spoken for, Aislinn? Betrothed? Mayhap already married?"

She blinked, suddenly uncomfortable. "Me?"

"Aye, *you*."

She shook her head fiercely. "Not married—and why would you ask such a thing?"

"Curious, is all—like you about Cameron. And the other? Are you betrothed?"

Again she shook her head, a lie jumping to her lips —for in her mind, she wasn't spoken for, no matter what plans her father might have for her.

"No! Now if you'll leave me, Conall Campbell," she

blurted, attempting again to shut the door. "And don't forget my clothes. A tunic and—"

"Trousers, aye. You're a strange one yourself, Aislinn De Burgh. A woman skilled with a sword and preferring tae dress like a man. No wonder you have my poor brother so flustered."

Conall retracted his boot so Aislinn could slam the door shut even as she heard him utter a low whistle—and then chuckle again.

She spun around and slumped with her back against the wall, her mind racing, her face burning. She had never been one for blushing and now she couldn't seem to stop.

Cameron flustered? What about her? Saints help her, what had come over her? Her father and her brother—aye, they should be the only ones occupying her mind.

Uttering a hardly feminine curse, she tore off the breacan and tossed it to the floor, though the scent of the man seemed to cling to her.

Cameron's scent.

She decided then and there that as soon as they brought her some clothes, she would ask for a hot bath, too, and scrub the smell of him from her—though at once, Aislinn felt a surge of remorse.

Finnegan had chastened her about her temper—but she had never known a red-haired Irishwoman without one. Yet if everything Conall had told her was true, she owed a great debt to Cameron for helping to save her life that she must repay.

Aye, there had to be something she could do—other than reining in her temper—to help him as well, but what?

CHAPTER 7

"I'll return within a week, Conall. Swear tae me you'll keep everything under control while I'm gone."

"Another oath this fine morning? The air is ringing with them," Conall answered with a wry smile, though he quickly sobered at Cameron's frown and nodded solemnly. "Aye, you have my word. A good thing that storm passed us by or you'd be riding in the mud tae Dumbarton. Take care, brother, and watch your sword around that one."

Conall's glance at Aislinn mounted behind him made Cameron stiffen—och, did he have to mention her stealing his weapon in the blink of an eye and using it against him? The day not turning out at all how he had planned, twenty armed men mounted as well and waiting astride their snorting horses, Cameron heaved a sigh and cast a look around the bailey.

It seemed everything had ground to a standstill, as warriors hard at their training and servants busy with chores stopped what they were doing to see them off, only a few hours since he'd been forced under duress to swear to Aislinn's demand to take her to King Robert.

A knife at Conall's throat, no less! Cameron still couldn't believe she had done such a thing—but then again, had anything about her been commonplace since he had first laid eyes upon her?

"Well, Laird Campbell, are we going to sit here or finally be on our way?"

Her impatient query grating upon him, Cameron didn't spare her a glance but focused once again upon Conall.

"If anything goes awry, send a messenger at once."

"Nothing will go awry, Cameron—and if it does, Gabriel is only a few hours' ride away. I'd be more likely tae seek his assistance than trouble you"—Conall stepped closer to Cameron's massive black steed—"since you've got your hands full enough, wouldna you agree?"

Again Cameron sighed, as much with resignation as frustration that this fool's errand would take him away from the fortress when he'd only been the laird for five days—God help him, less than a full week. Nodding to Conall, he raised his hand, signaling for those that accompanied him that the moment for them to take their leave had come.

Within those few hours of intense activity, everything and everyone needed for the journey had been assembled, Cameron feeling for the first time that he was truly in command over both the fortress and his Campbell clansmen.

Not a man questioning his orders.

Not a servant hesitating to assist in preparing the provisions that had been strapped to a half-dozen pack horses.

And thankfully—*finally!*—his two unwanted prospective brides had left ahead of them with their entourage, without Cameron having to utter a word of farewell.

Conall had bid them goodbye in the bailey with the diplomacy of a seasoned courtier, while Cameron had watched from a tower window, and then turned at once to shoving the last of what he needed into a leather bag.

All the while his thoughts captured by Aislinn—always Aislinn, though he had tried to thrust her from his mind.

She had been one of the first to mount up and wait for him outside the massive stable, her horse no calm and steady gelding, but a lively roan stallion that even now whinnied and tossed its head impatiently. Would she ever cease to amaze him?

A glance over his shoulder told him that Aislinn remained just as eager as she lifted her chin to stare boldly at him, which made Cameron snap his gaze back forward and gather up the reins.

Her retreat from death's door to sitting so capably astride one of the most high-spirited horses among his stock had astounded him as well, though the sharpness of her cheekbones and pale cast to her skin was still evidence of what she'd suffered. Thanks to the swift needle of a seamstress, she wore a close-fitting woolen tunic and trousers, and her leather shoes from the prison cell cleaned and thrust into the stirrups.

Conall, too, had been quite industrious in finding her a fur-trimmed cloak that Cora had left behind, as well as a leather belt around her waist that could sheathe a knife—but there Cameron had adamantly drawn the line, refusing to give her a weapon. *Any weapon*!

"Good journey, brother," shouted Conall as Cameron urged his mount into motion. Others watching echoed the sentiment, the bailey resounding with their voices as he and his men—and Aislinn—rode in a thunder of hooves out the fortress gates.

Good journey? An ordeal more like it, that he hoped would be over as quickly as he could manage and Lady De Burgh soon to become King Robert's problem—

"God bless you, Laird Campbell!" came a resounding

shout repeated by villagers who rushed from their homes and shops to wave and cheer as Cameron passed by.

The broad smiles on their faces were so different than days ago when he had ridden toward the fortress through the village that lay just outside those imposing walls.

Corpses hanging from trees and lying alongside the road, and the piteous sound of women weeping had been the cruel evidence of Earl Seoras lashing out at his own clansmen in his ill-fated quest to become king—och, thank God the man was dead.

Already the houses and side streets looked different, too, as if sunlight had burst through a black pall of despair. Doors and shutters were freshly white-washed and everything swept and tidied, his heart warmed by the sound of children playing and laughing.

Aye, he had so many responsibilities now, but if this was the result, then it was well worth his every effort to make life better for all those under his charge.

Cameron felt so encouraged by everything he saw that he even nodded to a trio of comely lasses who waved at him and curtsied, which would have shocked Conall from his horse if he'd seen it.

That thought sobered Cameron quickly enough—for Conall wasn't riding with him but left behind at the fortress to manage things, which only heightened Cameron's resolve to reach King Robert as soon as possible.

Not because he didn't trust Conall, but that he could feel Aislinn's gaze upon him. Cameron felt suddenly as uncomfortable as early that morning when she had demanded that he face her and speak to him.

His heart hammering. His throat constricted.

His eyes stinging from staring so intently into the fire until he had turned and looked at her, his gaze dropping to her breasts so full and saucy beneath a soaked nightgown that clung to her like a second skin.

At once he'd glanced at Conall, anger ripping through him to think that he had been gazing upon her as well. Yet Conall had been focused upon his porridge —och, Cameron hadn't liked at all feeling such resentment directed at his brother.

He had pulled off his breacan and tossed it at her almost without thinking, and Aislinn had covered herself, her cheeks flushed with what he imagined was chagrin.

Did she not realize how lovely she was, more so than any woman he had ever seen? Had she not seen the appreciative glances of his men moments ago, Cameron having all he could do not to reprimand them?

She might not wear feminine garb, but her tunic and trousers sewn to fit her lithe form left no doubt that she was a woman—unlike the loose-fitting clothing she'd been found in the day before.

Thankfully she had wrapped herself in binding again —by God, would he be tormented by thoughts of her beautiful breasts springing free the entire journey?

"You surprise me, Laird Campbell."

Cameron glanced with a start at Aislinn, who had ridden up beside him. Her spirited mount bumped into his steed, making both stallions squeal and shake their heads.

Only his tight grip on the reins kept his horse from rearing, while Aislinn gave a light laugh as if the mishap had amused her.

Yet Cameron wasn't amused, not at all, and wondered what the men following behind two by two must think of what they had just witnessed. Once again he made himself think of her as an opponent, for she could have cost him his seat—and mayhap his neck—if he hadn't been able to control his skittish steed.

"Get back behind me," he said gruffly, but Aislinn appeared to have no intention of heeding his command, and matched the trotting pace of his stallion.

"From everything Conall told me, I would not have thought you afflicted at all from the smile you gave those young women."

Smile? Cameron hadn't smiled at anyone, least of all any women, his hands tightening on the reins even as his throat tightened.

Conall had spoken to her about him? Afflicted? His gut clenching with intuition, he was glad that his brother wasn't riding with him for he might have cuffed him.

"I nodded at them, is all—now get back behind me."

"Aye, you speak quite easily to me when you're angry —but what about when you're not? I only want to help you, much as you've helped me. Why don't you think of me as a male like yourself and then mayhap you and I can talk—"

"*A male?*" Cameron roared, startling not only their horses, but the closest ones behind them. "Lady De Burgh, your garb does not make you look any more a man than I could pass for a woman—now will you heed me or shall we stop right here until you do?"

He got no answer, only a small shrug as she glanced at him with what he would swear was pity.

"There's no shame in your shyness around women, Laird Campbell—and just listen to you! Angry, aye, just as I said, and mayhap even thinking of me as some sort of enemy, which makes sense to me. I hope you can forgive me for taking your sword, but I thought you an enemy, too. Yet we're not enemies at all, both of us loyal to King Robert. I'm so grateful to you for taking me to him, and I want to make amends, Cameron. Will it trouble you if I call you by your given name?"

In truth, he didn't know what to say, the words spilling from her in a wild rush. Aislinn only shrugged at his silence and steered her mount closer, and she leaned closer to him, too, as if what she might say was for his ears alone.

"You see? I'm a woman and speaking to you—aye, looking at you—and lightning hasn't struck you down. The sky hasn't darkened and the earth hasn't opened up to swallow you. I'm certain that the more we talk to each other, the less uncomfortable you'll feel, and I promise I'll do my best not to snap at you—at least, I'll try not to. Sometimes my temper gets the better of me and I've been known to act without thinking—"

"Like pressing a knife tae my brother's throat?" Cameron demanded, his anger flaring hot again. *"Threatening his life?"*

"Aye, well, that surprised me, too, but look what I gained. We're on our way to King Robert and you're speaking to me—in anger, I'll admit, but it's a start. Finnegan always told me that it takes practice to become good at anything. How else do you think I became so skilled with the sword?"

Cameron bristled, still incredulous that she had bested him and come so close to wounding him—och, and let him not forget the candlestick to his head. He reached up to touch the sore spot, thankfully no deeper than a scratch, and saw Aislinn wince as if the cut had been her own.

"Mayhap you'll forgive me for that, too—*oh!*"

Her mount sidestepped so suddenly at a rabbit running across the road that Cameron had to grab her before she tumbled off—Aislinn's rump now wedged between his thighs even as she gasped in outrage.

"Could you not give me a chance to right myself?" she demanded while laughter erupted from the men riding behind them, making her face flare bright red as she twisted around to glare at him. "Stop at once and let me down. Let me down!"

Cameron thought to oblige her, but her indignant

wriggling made him wonder if he held her fast, mayhap she would cease her endless chatter and leave him in peace. Certain that if she'd had a knife sheathed in her belt, she would have pressed it to his own throat by now, he held her all the more tightly against him so that she couldn't struggle.

"Temper, Aislinn, temper," he grated, glad to have a chance to teach her a lesson. "I swore tae protect you, remember? What was I tae do? Let you fall and injure yourself?"

"I-I wouldn't have fallen," she sputtered, balling her fists and flailing her arms. Cameron quickly caught them and pinned them within his embrace, and now she really couldn't move, her rump wedged even more securely against him.

The sensation wholly new to him, to hold a woman so closely, Cameron swallowed hard at the heat rising in his loins—och, not the only thing rising.

Still his men chuckled behind him, a glance over his shoulder telling Cameron that one of them had grabbed the reins to Aislinn's mount, the stallion trotting along-side the man's horse.

Meanwhile she had grown ominously silent, which was exactly what he had wanted.

Damn Conall, to share with her something Cameron had never discussed with anyone! His own private pain. His own private torment. Had his men heard much of what she'd said over the clopping hooves? God help him, he hoped not.

Yet for the first time since boyhood, his tongue had not grown thick at what little he'd said to her—aye, her chatter distracting him in spite of his anger.

Would she refuse to honor his commands for the entire journey? If she had reined in her horse and fallen back as he had demanded, she wouldn't be seething in his arms—aye, for he sensed she was no doubt plotting how to best him.

Cameron knew he should call for her horse to be brought forward, if only to quell his men's amusement at her expense, which must be further infuriating her. Yet the warmth of her body was so stirring a sensation, one he'd never known before, that he could not bring himself to utter the order.

Her taut bottom flush against him—och, could a woman be so lithe and yet so wondrously rounded? Cameron felt his throat grow tight for another reason than the affliction that had so long plagued him.

His lower body swollen and rigid.

Desire like flame ripping through him.

The sun-warmed scent of her hair, her skin, overwhelming him.

Every motion of his steed driving the curve of her rump against him—och, God, had there ever been such sweet torment?

Aislinn had tensed, too, and seemed to tremble within his embrace, her head leaning back against his shoulder as if she'd given up on any thought to fight him.

She had grown so quiet... too quiet.

That realization made Cameron snap out of the daze that gripped him, as if he'd been doused with cold water—Aislinn at the same moment grabbing the reins from his hands to jerk upon them with all of her might.

Squealing, his horse reared.

Both of them sliding backward and tumbling to the ground with an astonished curse from Cameron and a shriek of outrage from Aislinn.

She rolled away from him and jumped to her feet with her fists clenched and her feet squarely planted, while Cameron rose to stare at her in awe.

Her blue eyes ablaze. Her cheeks flushed bright pink. Her expression more chagrined than infuriated as she seemed to fight to catch her breath.

His breath came hard, too, but one glance at his

men, who had stopped their horses and looked on in consternation, made Cameron recover himself.

He strode over to his horse, which tossed its head and nickered at him nervously, and calmed the creature enough so he could once again mount.

One of his men had brought Aislinn her steed and she had mounted, too, her expression unreadable but for the dark turbulence of her eyes.

Something had changed between them; Cameron could feel it as surely as he breathed, and he wondered if she felt it, too.

A fire burning brightly now, which he realized as they set out again, had been smoldering inside him from the moment he had first set eyes upon her.

Aislinn.

He could no longer leave her with King Robert, mayhap never to see her again, than he could deny that he wanted her.

Already within his heart, his mind, his very soul, Cameron had claimed her for his own.

And if winning her heart meant helping her find her father and brother, or at least what had happened to them, then aye, he would do it.

And if overcoming his affliction meant he must make himself speak to her as any man might to a lass, Cameron feeling truly hopeful for the first time in his life—*aye, he would do it*!

CHAPTER 8

A islinn had never felt so humiliated—aye, so much so that she had refused to utter a word to Cameron since that debacle when he had pulled her onto his horse.

Refused to meet his gaze whenever she felt him watching her, which seemed to be at every turn.

When they had stopped to water the horses or to eat from the provisions packed for them—salted venison, oatcakes, dried apples, and a crock of cold porridge that had been tasteless without any fresh cream.

When they had camped for a few hours last night at the rocky base of a bluff, a fire fed with gathered branches, grass, and twigs, keeping them warm against the cool night air. Aislinn and Cameron off to one side, while his men spread out on the other three sides and took turns sleeping and watching guard.

When Aislinn had gotten up from a tartan blanket spread upon the ground to venture a short way into the trees to relieve herself, Cameron's gaze hard upon her.

He had seemed disinclined to sleep, while she had finally allowed herself to rest after staring up into the star-filled sky, her eyes welling with tears.

Tears that she had tried to blink away in vain, the

moisture trickling down her cheeks as she had turned her face away from the fire.

Aye, her mortification so great that even now, on the second evening of their journey, Aislinn felt as if it might choke her.

The same tortured thoughts whirling in her mind and making her clench the reins in silent outrage.

She had offered to help Cameron in all sincerity with his affliction and yet what had he done? Seized upon the first opportunity to put her in her place—a woman's place!—while his men had laughed at her.

Laughed when Cameron had grabbed her from her horse and wedged her between his thighs... strong, muscular thighs that had been like a vise at her hips, his equally powerful arms holding her fast no matter how hard she struggled.

Laughed when Cameron continued to hold her when he could have easily called for her horse and released her.

God only knows what his men must have been thinking at the sight of Cameron clasping her so closely —saints help her, at least they were riding behind them in formation and couldn't see her face.

Her cheeks aflame at the stirring warmth she'd felt in Cameron's arms.

She had never been held in such a manner, her bottom jammed against his inner thighs while something rigid pressed her there—ah, God, she wasn't so naïve about men that she hadn't known exactly what was happening.

All the while, Cameron's breathing tickling her ear, not harsh but not steady, either, as he had drawn her even closer.

Her breathing unsteady, too, the strangest sensation coursing through her that she'd never known before... her mind screaming for him to let her go while her trembling body seemed to have betrayed her.

Now as she rode upon her own horse behind him, his broad back to her and his shoulders tense as if he sensed her watching him, Aislinn shivered.

Aye, right to her toes, just like the moment before she had pulled so fiercely on the reins and caused Cameron's steed to rear up on its hind legs—both of them toppling into the dirt.

That had made his men stop laughing, while Aislinn had resolved not to speak to Cameron ever again—aye, she couldn't wait until they reached the place where King Robert and his forces were quartered.

She had overheard Cameron talking to his men yesterday before they left the fortress that their destination was Dumbarton Castle, so recently held by the English but now in Scottish hands. The very place where William Wallace had been imprisoned before being taken to London and his grisly death—aye, they all knew in Éire of that courageous warrior's efforts to free his country from King Edward's tyranny.

Yet many in her homeland had despised Wallace—aye, those who held land and estates granted by the Crown. Many De Burghs were loyal to King Edward, while others, like her father, had chosen a different path and supported King Robert.

Just thinking about her family made Aislinn chew her lower lip.

She wished so desperately that they had arrived at the castle, but another night lay ahead of them—dusk already settling over the land. The craggy mountains to the north swathed in darkening hues of purple and blue, while the rolling hills in front of them were tinged with gold from the last warming rays of the sun.

Aye, another night where she would have to lie close to Cameron on one side of the fire while the men not standing guard grunted and snored in their sleep like pigs.

She knew she shouldn't think so ill of them, loyal as

they all were to King Robert, but after them laughing at her? If she'd had a knife at her belt, they wouldn't have been so amused, but blinking in surprise when she held the weapon to Cameron's throat—

"No camp tonight, I want tae press on tae Dumbarton," Cameron's brusque command broke into her mutinous thoughts, elation sweeping through Aislinn.

They must be close or he would stop, surely. Mayhap only a few more leagues away!

She had overheard him talking to his men yesterday as well that he'd traveled this route a few weeks ago with his former commander, Gabriel MacLachlan, when they had gone to fetch Gabriel's bride-by-proxy from a convent near Dumbarton.

By proxy? That meant the poor colleen hadn't been allowed to speak for herself, but was no doubt married against her will.

Saints preserve all women. Would the day ever come when their lot wouldn't be determined by men?

Sighing with frustration, Aislinn forced away the memory of Cameron's warriors laughing at *her* expense as he twisted around in the saddle to look at her.

"Do you need tae stop, Aislinn?"

She bristled, his query not brusque at all but uttered in so even-tempered a manner that she wondered again if she was being addressed by the same man.

So he had done since yesterday, each time no more than a brief comment or question, and she had refused to acknowledge a one of them.

Lay your blanket there, Aislinn.

Would you like another oatcake?

Time tae wake, Aislinn.

That last one had wholly startled her, Cameron kneeling beside her and gently shaking her shoulder with no hint of the affliction Conall had told her about.

His voice so low and husky that she had shivered then, too, but at once she had jumped to her feet and whisked up her blanket. Aislinn astonished by the change in him as he had looked at her so strangely...

"No! I don't need to stop," she retorted in spite of her resolve not to speak to him, her mind racing again.

Whatever had come over the man? Had he decided to take to heart what she'd said to him after all—that it took practice to become good at anything? Had he forgiven her as well for taking a weapon to both him and Conall, and his anger had cooled? Mayhap speaking to her in so calm a manner was his attempt to make amends for what had happened yesterday...

"My thanks, though," Aislinn muttered, still not able to fully let go of the embarrassment he had caused her. As if astonished that she had softened her tone, he glanced at her over his shoulder, but she averted her eyes—a sudden sound in the distance making the hair prickle at the back of her neck.

A scream, aye, there it was again!

A high-pitched, feminine outcry of such terror and distress that Aislinn's horse snorted and tossed his head, while Cameron and his men acted like they hadn't even heard it.

Or had they? She saw that Cameron's shoulders had stiffened and he glanced in the direction of the scream —until another shriek of such fright made her jerk hard upon the reins and kick her horse into a gallop.

"*Aislinn!*"

Cameron had bellowed out her name, but she didn't stop—how could she?

Not with the screams growing louder, Aislinn plunging her mount through the trees as dusk deepened around her.

She heard the pounding of hooves not far behind and knew Cameron and his men followed, but she pressed forward until she burst into a clearing brightened by a sputtering torch thrust between two branches.

75

Three soldiers dressed in mail shirts who had been kneeling upon the ground jumped to their feet to stare at her wide-eyed, though a second more and they had drawn their swords.

Aislinn's heart in her throat as she recognized them as English from their conical helmets and knee-length gray tunics—the same garb she'd seen on the beach where her father and Daran had been attacked.

Was there a larger force nearby? She could smell salt air on the stiff breeze and knew they weren't far from water. Mayhap they'd come from a stronghold that hadn't yet fallen to King Robert?

Her horse whinnying sharply as the men surrounded her, Aislinn had only to glance at the bedraggled girl lying upon the ground who wept piteously to know what the bastards had been about.

Saints help her, how was she to defend herself without a knife or sword? Pulling hard on the reins, she made her horse rear with hooves pawing the air—which scattered the soldiers until she realized Cameron had ridden up beside her.

Everything happened so swiftly as he jumped to the ground and attacked the soldiers with his sword glinting in the torchlight, two of the men cut down before she had drawn a breath.

Before she'd even realized his warriors had ridden into the clearing, though none of them had dismounted.

The third soldier throwing down his weapon and falling to his knees in terror at the fearsome sight of Cameron coming toward him, Aislinn in awe, too.

His sword lifted.

His countenance truly ominous to behold as he slowly lowered the weapon and used the bloodstained blade to lift the man's trembling chin.

"Out for an evening tumble?"

Aislinn had never heard such quiet fury in

Cameron's voice—not at all his usual bluster—while the soldier pissed himself, staining his tunic, and wildly shook his head.

"N-not me, lord! The others!"

"Och, so you were just going tae watch as they defiled the lass—mayhap awaiting your turn. *Where did you find her?*"

Now Cameron had roared, making the soldier begin to sob as he gestured to the west, the blade still pressed beneath his chin.

"Her home, lord, not far from here."

"Tell me you didna slay her family—"

"No-no, we just took the girl—and the calf there, for our supper."

Indeed, a wee bawling calf had been tied crosswise to a shaggy pony—the poor creature only a few days old, Aislinn judged.

Unable to hold back any longer, she slid from the saddle and ran to the girl—God in heaven, no more than twelve, Aislinn was certain of it—who had rolled onto her side and curled up into a ball.

"Here... let me help you."

In the background she could hear Cameron speaking in a low, menacing voice to the soldier, but Aislinn paid them no heed as she drew the sobbing girl into her arms to hug her.

"I heard you screaming," she said softly, Aislinn's heart aching as she tried to soothe her by wiping the light blond hair from her ashen face. "I rode here as fast as I could. Did they...?"

The jerky shake of the girl's head made such relief sweep through Aislinn that tears burned her eyes, and she glanced at Cameron to see him standing there, watching her.

The soldier on his feet and still breathing, which made her certain that the man must have revealed something to Cameron that made him spare his life.

For the time being.

Cameron's expression still so ominous that Aislinn felt a chill.

"She wasn't... they didn't—" she began, but he merely strode forward and swept up the girl into his arms.

"Let's take her home tae her family."

Aislinn nodded and rose beside him, watching as he carried the girl to his horse and lifted her onto his saddle.

So gently.

So carefully, which made Aislinn remember as if from a dream when she had been too weak to open her eyes and someone had picked her up and carried her— aye, with steady, strong arms—before blackness had claimed her.

Cameron...

CHAPTER 9

"You could have been killed."

His hands clenched at his sides, Cameron had not yet relaxed from battle as Aislinn stared at him with defiance, her stunning eyes a dark blue in the firelight.

The grateful parents of the girl who had come so close to defilement had begged for him and his men to camp outside their sod-roofed house for the night, and he had reluctantly agreed.

He had tried to assure them that no other English soldiers were near. The two men that he'd slain and the third one that sat huddled against a tree, trussed up and stinking of urine, had found themselves driven off course by rough currents, lost.

Their rowboat abandoned along a nearby inlet, they had stumbled upon the small farm and helped themselves to bread and ale, a pony, a calf, and the parents' only child, their thirteen-year-old daughter. All taken upon threat of death if they resisted, Cameron still amazed that the soldiers hadn't slaughtered the father and mother who had been beside themselves with grief.

At least until Cameron and his men and Aislinn had ridden up with the girl, who had broken into fresh weeping at first sight of her parents.

79

Their tearful reunion had made Cameron send up a swift prayer of thanks for an outcome that would have been far more brutal if the girl hadn't screamed so desperately—Aislinn veering her horse into the woods just as he'd pulled on the reins to do the same.

God help him, and her with no weapon to wield!

Cameron could not get out of his mind the sight of the soldiers raising their swords to strike at her just as he had thundered into the clearing. The fools had no doubt believed her a man, aye, and why wouldn't they?

Aislinn dressed in her male garb and with cropped hair, and astride a horse more snorting beast than a reliable mount—and yet with no weapon.

Sighing heavily, Cameron unsheathed the knife at his belt and handed it to her, not surprised that her gaze widened.

"Take it. I'll not have you without a means tae protect yourself if you defy me again, which I'm certain will happen. By God, woman, *why are you the way you are?*"

He stood with her away from his men—most of them already bedding down around the fire while others stood guard—and wasn't surprised, either, that she didn't readily respond to his fierce whisper.

Instead she grabbed the knife as if thinking he might change his mind, and slid the weapon into her own belt, and then lifted her chin at him.

"Why are *you* the way you are? If you can answer me that, Cameron Campbell, then mayhap I'll answer *your* query. One moment afflicted and then the next, you're not? Aye, it's clear that you're speaking to me right now because you're furious—but what else could I do? You didn't seem in a hurry to help—"

"You beat me tae it by no more than a blink, Aislinn. Do you think so ill of me that I wouldna heed such cries?"

Cameron didn't wait for her to answer, but took her

by the arm and led her further away, not wanting his men to overhear anything else from them.

Now he *was* surprised that she didn't resist him, but instead looked up into his face as if what he'd said had startled her.

"I... I don't think ill of you," she began, but then she pulled her arm away. "Go on, then, will you answer me?"

She was daring him, Cameron knew it, even as he felt a heaviness in his tongue that he had been fighting against since yesterday. Conversing with her when he was fuming was one thing, but now with her standing so close, his anger was cooling in spite of himself.

She looked so beautiful in the light cast by the fire.

She smelled like fresh air and smoke and a hint of something so captivating that he'd come to recognize as simply—Aislinn.

He had kept his every spoken interaction with her brief for fear that he might jumble his words and make himself look a fool—but she was staring at him and demanding a response. Mayhap if he fanned his anger again by thinking of her riding so rashly into danger—

"Just as I thought. It's more *you* thinking ill of me that you have so little to say."

She turned from him as if to walk away, but Cameron caught her by the elbow.

"Aislinn... it's hard for me tae speak tae women. I dinna know why. It's the way God made me... ever since I was a wee boy."

There, it was done and admitted to for the first time in his life. Cameron felt his throat growing tight as she turned back to face him, her expression unreadable.

He shrugged, not knowing what else to say. He didn't feel unmanned, just suddenly very weary as he wondered if she might now think him less than whole.

Aye, he had felt less than whole as long as he could remember, but what was to be done about it? He had never cared what women thought of him... until Aislinn. Aye, he cared about what might be going through her mind, more than he could say—

"So you're crippled by shyness, Cameron. It's an unfortunate malady and I'm sure you've suffered, but at least you weren't born a woman. Always fighting to be heard. To be seen..."

He heard a break in her voice and saw tears glistening in her eyes, but she appeared to blink them back and raised her chin.

"My mother told me that my father wept when I was born, not being a son. He had little to do with me... almost as if I wasn't there. One of my first memories is him patting me on the head, a rare acknowledgement, and then walking away. Always walking away. Yet when my brother, Daran, was born three years later, the house rang with my father's joy. He had his son. He hardly spoke to me from that moment on..."

Now her voice was shaking and she looked away, her lovely profile limned in firelight.

Cameron could feel his heart beating harder that she had shared so much with him, her lower lip trembling as she seemed to fight anew what must have been a terrible reality—in her mind at least. Yet was her lot so different than most highborn young women? Aye, some with fathers that might have showed fondness towards a daughter, but wasn't it always the sons that insured a man's lineage?

As if Aislinn had read his thoughts, her voice was bitter as once again, she turned away from him.

"I should have known you wouldn't understand. Why would you? You're a man like any other."

She started to walk back toward the fire, but Cameron caught up with her and with one hand at her waist, turned her around to face him. She didn't resist him this time, either, but he could tell by the tension in her body that she wasn't pleased about him stopping her.

"Didn't you tell your men that we'd be leaving at sunrise? I need some rest, Cameron—"

"Aye, but talk with me for a while longer, will you? You told me yourself that it might help—and I believe it has. You see? I'm not angry any longer and I'm trying, Aislinn, truly trying..."

Indeed he was, Cameron astonished at himself that he had spoken so easily to her, though his neck was sweating in spite of the cool night air.

Mayhap revealing what he'd never spoken aloud to anyone, not even Conall, had eased the affliction that had plagued him for so long—though more likely, it was because he wanted to talk with Aislinn.

To be near her.

To look into her eyes.

To find out more about her, though she sighed as if reluctant to say anything more to him. How could he blame her? Mayhap if he gently prodded her...

"So your father is why you're the way you are? A woman more skilled with a sword than many a man I've met in battle. More skilled with a horse—aye, that brute you ride has tossed most others who've tried tae tame him."

"You as well?"

Cameron heard a hint of humor in her voice that heartened him more than he could have imagined. He shook his head, and then shrugged.

"I have my own steed, a gift from Gabriel after he agreed tae wed Earl Seoras's mad sister, Magdalene. He gave each of his captains a fine horse—myself, Conall, and two others, Alun and Finlay—"

"She was mad?"

Cameron shook his head again at her startled look. "She feigned lunacy so she wouldna have tae marry— och, she led poor Gabriel on a merry chase, but now they couldna be happier. You'd like her, Aislinn. You remind me of her—strong, spirited, a mind of her own. Mayhap one day you'll have a chance tae meet her."

Smiling to himself at the memory of some of Magdalene's wild antics, Cameron grew sober in the next moment as he realized Aislinn was staring at him.

Almost in wonder. He realized then that he'd never spoken so easily and so much to anyone but Conall and Gabriel and his fellow captains, which made him suddenly fumble and grasp for words.

"I-I dinna know why I'm going on... och, you said you wanted tae rest—"

"It's working, Cameron, don't stop on my account. I told you if you practiced, it would get better. I said I'd help you and I meant it."

Cameron didn't know if it was her encouragement that so warmed him or that she had rested her hand upon his, her unexpected touch like a jolt that made him want to pull her into his arms.

He had no more thought of doing just that when she dropped her hand as if embarrassed, and once again looked toward the fire.

"It's getting late, aye?"

He nodded, fumbling again as his breath seemed jammed in his chest. "I-I'll walk you back..."

I'll walk you back? Was that all Cameron could think to say after everything that had passed between them?

Tomorrow by midday they would reach Dumbarton Castle, and who knew what Robert the Bruce might want to do with Aislinn? Cameron planned to insist upon his helping her himself to find her father and brother, or at least discover their fate—but he had been ordered by the king only days ago to remain at Campbell Castle to ensure the MacDougalls didn't attempt to wrest back control of Argyll.

What would King Robert have to say about Cameron disobeying that order? About Conall left in charge of so important a fortress?

"Cameron... I thank you for the knife."

He blinked, the two of them already back to the fire while his thoughts had run away with him. She didn't wait for a reply, but was already busying herself with arranging her blanket to one side like they had done the night before, Cameron's gut clenching.

Would they be parted tomorrow? Was she eager to be rid of him when he could not imagine a day without her?

Regretting his anger, and regretting that he hadn't praised her bravery and said so many other things that might have pleased her, including what he had learned from their prisoner, Cameron cursed under his breath.

Aislinn at once glanced up at him from where she'd lain down, her expression teasing as she drew a flap of the blanket over her.

"If you're thinking you might be in danger during the night, I promise I won't use the blade against you."

With that, she rolled onto her side with her back to the fire, Cameron certain that he heard her chuckling softly to herself.

Women! What did he know about them—other than not much at all? Wishing he'd paid more heed to Conall's practiced tactics when it came to wooing lasses, aye, his brother's aim solely to bed them, Cameron knew that wasn't how he thought of Aislinn De Burgh.

He wanted to wed her. His clan had made it clear that he must take a bride, and he had found the only one he could imagine becoming his wife.

The only woman who had made him speak as if he had no affliction at all—Cameron feeling whole for the first time in his life.

Staring at her still, his heart thundering, his hope growing, he had all he could do to lie down upon his blanket and attempt to go to sleep.

If he reached out his arm, he would even be able to

touch her—och, but he didn't want to lose his fingers, no matter what she'd said.

She was armed now, which gave him some comfort that she wouldn't be defenseless if any danger came upon them.

Or if she rushed headlong into peril again—God help him, was there any doubt of it?

CHAPTER 10

"That man knows something of my father?" Stunned, Aislinn looked from Cameron to the English soldier who had been hoisted onto one of the pack horses, his hands tied behind him and a rag stuffed in his mouth.

"Not of Lord De Burgh... only that prisoners held for ransom in Scotland will be moved tae Carlisle where King Edward has amassed his forces. He must have learned of recent captures from his spies and wants the gold in his coffers—not those of nobles who owe him their land and estates. Then he'll have the prisoners executed."

"You said this is good news?" Her cheeks burning, Aislinn stared in disbelief at Cameron, who solemnly nodded his head.

"Aye, as good as can be hoped for. The prisoners will be out in the open and not locked away in a dungeon where they canna be reached. At least this way, if your father and brother are still alive, there will be a chance tae rescue them."

"Still alive..." Disheartened now more than she could say in spite of Cameron's surprising revelation, and with the porridge she'd eaten sitting like a lump in her stomach, Aislinn lashed out at him. "Why didn't you tell me this last night? You could have, you know—"

"And risk you running over tae the prisoner and pointing your knife at his throat? At least with me telling you now, we got some rest without you demanding we ride out at once in the dark. You would have, you know, dinna deny it!"

Cameron's ire up—aye, anger always made him speak so easily—and his eyes darkened to a stormy blue, Aislinn did grasp the hilt of her knife as she glanced at the soldier.

The man must have been listening for he looked back at her with widened eyes, his face gone white.

"What else did he say? There had to be more."

"Aye, he and the other two were ordered tae deliver King Edward's edict tae a stronghold along the Firth of Clyde, but they were swept off course. A MacGodfrey stronghold rumored to have Irish prisoners—"

"MacGodfrey?" Aislinn broke in, a chill running through her. "The De Burghs are kin to that clan. One of them convinced my father to sail to Scotland in support of King Robert—Clive was his name... ah, God."

She fell silent while Cameron looked at her grimly, shaking his head.

"MacGodfreys were among Earl Seoras's courtiers, many of them slain. I released the few that still lived, an act of mercy, but I should have killed them all. They must have plotted with Earl Seoras tae capture your father and share the ransom. The most valuable prisoners taken tae the nearest stronghold, while the rest of you tae Seoras as proof of the ambush."

Aislinn winced as memories of that stinking black pit assailed her, but something did not yet make sense. She glanced at the soldier, who still eyed her nervously. "Cameron, some of those attackers were English and dressed much like that one—"

"Aye, I wouldna be surprised if that MacGodfrey stronghold is filled with English soldiers—since that clan has its nose stuck so far up King Edward's arse. Your father trusted the wrong man. Blood isna always thicker than water when it comes tae gold—och, enough, we must go."

Aislinn nodded, not offended at all that Cameron had spoken so bluntly, while he cast a dark look at the prisoner.

"Those fools should have stayed by their boat and gone back out onto the water at first light, but their empty bellies and lust gained us some time. When they dinna return tae their garrison, more soldiers will be sent out tae the stronghold, and whoever is in command will have no choice but tae obey the edict. Except now we'll be lying in wait along the road tae Carlisle with a wee surprise for them—"

"*We?*"

"Of course, you'll have tae ride along with us. How else will we know if your father and brother are among the prisoners?"

Astonished, Aislinn could only gape at Cameron as he signaled for his men to mount up.

Already the cloudless sky was brightening. They had risen before dawn to steaming hot porridge with cream and fresh baked bread served to them by the farmer and his wife, who couldn't stop thanking them.

The family stood now in the doorway to their modest home, but as soon as Aislinn moved to her horse, the girl named Sorcha came running to give her a hug.

"Thank you, Lady De Burgh, thank you!"

Aislinn hugged her back, hard, all the while praying that no more English soldiers would trouble them as Sorcha spun around and threw her arms around Cameron.

He looked so nonplussed for a moment that Aislinn

almost laughed, but that wouldn't do at all when he was trying so hard to overcome his affliction.

"Go on now—and God be with you and your parents," he murmured to the girl, who bobbed her head, her blue eyes alight, and ran back to the house with her golden hair flying.

Aye, if Cameron kept on as he was doing, there would be no sign left of the crippling shyness that had plagued him since boyhood—his sudden smile at Aislinn making her heart skip a beat.

Had a man ever been born so handsome?

The look he gave her alone would melt any woman's heart—a warmth in his eyes that sent familiar shivers coursing through her as he came closer and reached out his hand.

"Let me help you."

She thought to say that she could mount her steed by herself, but something made her hold her tongue and nod.

Ever since she had watched him carry Sorcha to his horse, so kindly, so gently... awakening that memory in Aislinn of Cameron holding her the same way though she must have reeked from that horrible pit—aye, she couldn't help but look at him differently.

As his hands, strong and sure, encircled her waist to lift her up onto the saddle, she could not deny that her resentment toward him after he'd pulled her onto his horse was gone altogether.

She saw now so clearly that he hadn't meant to humiliate her in front of his men, but prevent her from falling and hurting herself—just as he had said.

And when he'd given his own knife to her last night, even though he was still angry at her for riding off into the woods, she could hardly believe it.

Even moments ago, when she had snapped at him, provoking his frustration, she couldn't deny that he'd been right about her reaction to his news. If she had known last night about everything the prisoner had revealed to him, she would have insisted they set out at once for Dumbarton, no time to waste—

"You look pale, Aislinn." Cameron's concerned voice broke into her thoughts as he gazed up at her, handing her the reins. "It's still so soon after everything you suffered. Would you rather ride with me the rest of the way?"

Again, her first impulse was to retort that she was fine and could ride her own horse—aye, Finnegan had been right about her temper—but she simply shook her head.

"I'm fine, Cameron, truly. Don't worry for me—"

"Woman, I've done nothing but worry since the first time I saw you," he said with such candor that she felt a lump rise in her throat. A sudden fierceness burned in his eyes as he added, "If you hear any more screams, dinna ride off by yourself, Aislinn. Will you promise me?"

She didn't readily answer, her first instinct to say that she had his knife to protect her now, but something so earnest in his expression stilled her tongue and made her nod.

"No, you must say it."

"Aye, I promise."

He seemed to exhale slowly as if he'd been holding his breath, but then he nodded, too, and turned from her to stride to his horse.

Something so intense having passed between them that Aislinn couldn't even name it, though she felt it in her heart.

A tug. A pull, her eyes meeting Cameron's as he mounted and gestured for her to ride beside him—not behind him.

Side by side. To keep a closer watch upon her? Or to be nearer to her?

Suddenly breathless, Aislinn steered her horse toward him even as she knew from the way he looked at her, that it was the latter—and she wanted it, too.

To be nearer to him... and she had never felt that before for any man.

Especially not the one her father had chosen for her husband—saints help her, she didn't want to think about that unwanted arrangement.

She would choose her own husband one day, Aislinn wondering if Cameron had any say in those prospective brides coming to Campbell Castle.

He couldn't have escaped the great hall any faster, so she doubted it. A landed baron with no wife—aye, she could well imagine that his clan would wish to see him wed, and quickly.

That thought gave Aislinn a pang, which made her sigh and cast a glance at Cameron.

He glanced at her, too, locking eyes with her as they rode away from the farm, his men falling into formation behind them.

No hint of reticence at all in his gaze, but an intensity that made her heart beat faster as Conall's words came flying back to her.

Mayhap you're the cure he's been praying for...

She had pondered them last night, too, unable to fall asleep for a long time—and it wasn't only because Cameron lay so close to her, aye, only an arm's length away.

Everything they had shared with each other had astonished her... Aislinn still surprised at herself for telling him about her father's indifference.

Still surprised that Cameron had given his knife to her and told her about his secret pain since childhood.

Saints preserve him, no one would ever suspect from looking at the man that conversing with women or even being around them was so difficult for him. Yet he seemed to be trying so hard to overcome a wretched plight that no one should suffer—least of all as for-midable a warrior as Laird Cameron Campbell.

Aye, he wasn't only trying hard—but had praised her skill with the sword unlike anyone had done before. *Praised her*!

Only Finnegan—a trusted captain long in her fa-ther's service who had pitied her for his disinterest and agreed to teach her about weapons—had paid her any compliments, though he'd critiqued her far more often.

Your life will depend upon it, Aislinn, you must do better.

Hold the sword thus, aye, now thrust before they have a chance to kill you.

Lift your shield higher, Aislinn, aye, that's it!

Her skill with horses had come naturally since she was a girl, but Cameron had commended her for that, too.

Then he'd said Aislinn reminded him of Gabriel MacLachlan's wife, Magdalene, a woman whom he clearly admired and considered strong, spirited, and with a mind of her own. Aislinn had dreamed of hearing such praise from her father, but instead it had come from a man whom she had only known for a handful of days—

"How is it that you're not married, Aislinn?"

Her breath caught. She couldn't have been more startled than if Cameron had once again yanked her onto his horse. Her face burned, too, as Cameron seemed to note her discomposure.

"Forgive me. Conall said he asked you if you were married or betrothed—"

"Aye, he did, and I told him no," Aislinn cut him off, her voice shrill to her ears and her steed's as well, the stallion snorting and tossing his head. She eased her tightened grip on the reins even as Cameron edged his mount closer.

"It wasna my intent tae upset you, but you told me last night that your brother was born three years after you. Did your father take a raw youth with him into battle?"

"Daran is nearly eighteen and no raw youth—"

"Ah, so that makes you nearly twenty-one and well past the age when most highborn women are married."

"I told you my father paid me little heed, which in that respect, was fine with me. He was forever busy with matters of his estate or traveling to Dublin, taking my brother with him, and my mother died long ago."

"Och, God rest her. So you were left by yourself and Finnegan stepped in?"

"Aye, he did... because I begged him to teach me how to fight. It was only within the last few weeks before leaving for Scotland that my father took notice, mayhap what would become of me if he didn't return..." Aislinn fell silent, wondering why Cameron was asking her these probing questions. At that moment, she almost wished he wasn't speaking so much to her as he seemed to study her—

"Has your hair always been short?"

His voice so husky that she found herself blushing, Aislinn shook her head and gestured toward her waist.

"That long, then. It must have been beautiful."

She shrugged, though the way he was looking at her made her shiver anew. "I had to cut it to pass for a youth. The plans had been made, and my father and his men soon sailing to Scotland. Stowing away was the only way for me to go with them. Mayhap if he still lives and I'm able to help him, he'll see me differently. Listen to me. All I ask for is a say over my own life..."

"Aye, a say over one's life."

Cameron's voice grown somber, Aislinn swallowed hard at everything she had revealed to him—but not all.

He hadn't asked her if she was spoken for, but if she was married, and she had told him the truth. The other didn't matter, not unless her father refused her request

—saints help her, she didn't even know if he was yet alive to consider such an outcome.

All she knew was that soon they would arrive in Dumbarton and she'd come face-to-face with King Robert the Bruce. Her cousin's husband... and most likely, the man who—at least in the short term—would decide her fate.

Cameron clearly intended to help her find her father—the most astonishing surprise of all! Yet would she be allowed to accompany him?

Aislinn gave a low laugh, astonished that she would even consider such a thing.

Allow her? Even if the king said no, she would find a way. If her father still lived, she *must* help to rescue him. She had wanted to show him that she could fight, aye, as ably as a man, but the ambush had changed everything. Mayhap now she would have a second chance to prove herself and earn the right to choose her own future—

"Something amused you?"

Aislinn met Cameron's eyes, but the last thing she'd admit was any thought to defy King Robert. Instead she shrugged. "Sorcha hugging you, is all. You looked so startled, but it was kind, what you said to her. You're a good and honorable man, Laird Campbell—even if you do roar a bit too much."

"Roar?"

"Aye, and well you know it. Do all Highland lairds bellow and bluster like you?"

She was teasing him, and now he looked startled again, as if he couldn't believe it.

Yet a slow smile spread across his face as he gazed at her, making Aislinn's heart race... until he focused once more upon the low hills in the distance and urged his horse into a canter.

CHAPTER 11

"So you stowed aboard your father's ship. An impulsive and foolish move for a young woman"— King Robert shook his head as he scrutinized Aislinn's male garb—"even if I can see how you might pass for a youth. Thank God the ruse succeeded or you wouldna be standing before me now. I dinna want tae think of what Earl Seoras's men might have done tae you if they had discovered the truth."

Aislinn swallowed hard, not wanting to think of such a fate, either, while Cameron stood silently beside her.

So close that their fingers might have touched if she moved her hand just the slightest wee bit, but she stood stock-still as Robert the Bruce began to pace in front of them.

His footfalls the only sound in an antechamber leading into the great hall of Dumbarton Castle, though the din of the midday meal could be heard beyond the closed door.

To Aislinn, he looked as much a king as she could have imagined, strongly built and taller than most men —though Cameron towered over him by a head—with dark brown hair that brushed his muscular neck. His stride exuded power, his broad forehead creased in thought as if considering what Cameron had requested of him.

To allow her to accompany him to rescue her father and brother—*if* they still lived and could be rescued. That dark thought pressed in upon her as King Robert stopped to look at her with no small amount of disapproval.

"Do you underestimate for a moment, Lady De Burgh, what atrocities the English are capable of? What tyranny we've suffered under King Edward's yoke? My dear wife Elizabeth, *your own cousin*, is held prisoner in Yorkshire under frightful conditions and God alone knows when I will see her again. Yet you wish tae join my newly appointed baron on a perilous quest tae find your father, who, if wounded two weeks ago, is probably dead unless his captors afforded him a healer—*och*, woman! I can only think that Laird Campbell must be smitten with you tae ask such a thing of me—"

"Aye, my king, you have judged me rightly," Cameron broke in, though he bowed his head in deference. Yet only for an instant before he looked up to face Robert the Bruce, while Aislinn felt her cheeks ablaze. "It is my hope tae wed her, though I've not yet broached the matter with her... if she'll have me and if her father agrees—I mean, if he's alive—"

"I know what you meant, Campbell."

King Robert fell silent and looked again at Aislinn, who felt as if the floor could have opened up and swallowed her and she wouldn't have felt more astonished.

Cameron had not yet broached the matter with her? She couldn't bring herself to glance at him, but she jumped when she felt him suddenly clasp her fingers.

His fingers so strong and warm, which made her face burn hotter.

Ah, God, was this happening? One moment they had been awaiting King Robert's decision as to their plan, and now Cameron had spoken of his intent to ask for her hand in marriage?

She seemed to hear naught else but her pounding heartbeat, and still she could not bring herself to look at him.

Meanwhile, King Robert heaved a sigh, glancing at Cameron and back to her again. "Well, Lady De Burgh, what say you tae this revelation? If you're in agreement and will have Laird Campbell as your husband—of course, which canna be decided until we know the fate of your father and brother, then I wouldna refuse you accompanying him—"

"I agree, my lord king!" The words sprung from her mouth, Aislinn did glance now at Cameron to find him appearing as astonished as she had felt a moment ago. Yet his look of surprise vanished as he met her eyes and squeezed her hand, which made Aislinn feel suddenly as if she could not draw breath.

Cameron wanted her for his bride—saints above, was this truly happening? They had hardly spoken again during the ride to Dumbarton, as if his mind had been upon countless other matters. Then upon their arrival at the castle, they had been ushered at once into the antechamber to await the king.

She had been nervous, aye, but hopeful, too, Cameron telling her in a low aside to allow him to speak to King Robert, which had made her bristle. Yet the man had cut so imposing a figure when he'd entered the room that she had remained silent while Cameron explained how Aislinn had come to be with him, why he had left the fortress, and what he had heard from the English soldier about Irish prisoners at the Mac-Godfrey stronghold.

All the while King Robert had looked from one to

the other, listening intently, his expression sometimes inscrutable and then darkening and then impassive again until here they were now—Aislinn's head spinning.

Cameron wanted her for his bride! Still she had not torn her gaze from his, until King Robert cleared his throat and gave a wry chuckle.

"First Gabriel MacLachlan with his lunatic bride... and now my baron with his hoped-for bride posing as a youth. Both clever and courageous young women—but these are dangerous times, Laird Campbell."

"Aye, my lord king."

"You'll answer tae me—and mayhap her father—if any ill befalls her. I dinna doubt your resolve tae protect her, but Lady De Burgh would be safer remaining here while you attempt a rescue. Bear in mind that Clive MacGodfrey's prisoners might already have been taken tae Carlisle—"

"Clive is the laird there?" Aislinn blurted as Cameron's hand tightened around hers. "Forgive me, my lord. He's the one who encouraged my father to come fight for you—and who betrayed him. A Scots cousin on my mother's side."

"Aye, his stronghold's out of the way and lacking in importance tae our fight against Edward—so now isna the time tae lay siege. Hold tae your plan, Campbell, and position your men alongside the road tae Carlisle. I'll wager these prisoners will be well guarded, so I'll send twenty more soldiers with you. If Lord De Burgh and his son are among them, attack swiftly and then retreat tae Dumbarton. Clive would be a fool tae try and follow after—och, but I've battled such fools before."

Cameron nodded and Aislinn swallowed hard as once again, King Robert settled his piercing gaze upon her.

"Dinna do anything foolish, lass, do you understand

me? Stay close tae Laird Campbell and do exactly as he says. Mayhap you dinna know that he's one of the most formidable warriors in the land—and I thank God that he, Gabriel, and Conall saved my life only days ago. Has he told you what Earl Seoras had planned for me as part of the night's entertainment?"

"No, lord, not yet."

"Och, it seems he has quite a bit tae share with you —but no matter. If Seoras ordered you and your kinsmen dumped into a stinking pit, may God rest them, then you can well imagine my end was so close I could taste it. I would have felt the executioner's blade right there in the great hall of what is now Campbell Castle if not for Gabriel's wife recognizing me—"

"Magdalene, aye, I've heard about her," Aislinn interjected, King Robert clearly not minding at all as he chuckled again.

"Mad Maggie, they called her—though I could have told Gabriel she was no lunatic after I rescued her and the nuns a year past, when English soldiers attacked their convent. She would have fought tae the death tae protect those women—och, I'm going on when there's a fine luncheon awaiting us in the hall. Will you eat before you set out, Laird Campbell?"

Aislinn hoped so, her stomach rumbling, but Cameron shook his head, his voice grim.

"We need tae be on our way. MacGodfrey's prisoners mayhap will be bound for Carlisle by morning if more soldiers have been sent tae alert him tae Edward's edict."

"Damn him and his greed! Forever lining his coffers with ill-gotten gain, and even then, he'll order those wretched men hanged, drawn, and quartered—"

"Ah, God." Sickened by the thought of such a terrible fate for her father and brother, Aislinn swallowed against the bile that had tempered her hunger, while the king looked at her with great sternness.

"Stay close tae Laird Campbell, lass."

"Aye, I will. I promise."

"Good. You will need your own sword if you're as skilled with weapons as he says you are"—the king glanced at Cameron—"so see that she has one before you leave."

"Aye, my lord king."

"One more thing, Campbell. I'm giving you a week, and then you'll return tae the fortress whether or not her father and brother have been found. I need you there, not here, though it's an admirable quest... if only tae win her favor. Mayhap your clan willna be pleased if you take an Irish lass tae wife and not one of our own, but I'll stand by your choice if you have need of me."

As Cameron bowed his head again to the king, uttering his thanks, Aislinn felt her face burning even hotter than before.

If only tae win her favor...

Why had it not occurred to her that might be behind Cameron's desire to help her find her father? All she had to do was think upon how he'd held her, wedged between his thighs, his breath so warm against her ear and making her tremble... to know that something in that moment had forever changed between them.

She had felt it, and he certainly must have felt it from how he had stared at her afterward, his gaze always upon her.

Cameron doing his best to try and overcome his affliction and talk to her.

Cameron always so close to her... just as he was, even now. His hand still clasping hers, the strength in his fingers alone making her shiver.

"Ah, yes, when you return home, tell Conall that I havena forgotten him for his part in saving my life," King Robert said, as he walked with them to the door. "Leaving him in command of the fortress is a fine test of his mettle. He'll have his own estate one day when he accomplishes the task I'm considering for him. Yet the time isna right, not until midsummer—och, but enough."

Throwing open the door to the clamor of a great hall filled with his men at their midday meal, King Robert reached out to clasp Cameron's shoulder.

"Go with God, Campbell."

For Aislinn, the king gave only another stern look and then left them standing outside the antechamber, a great cheer resounding from the rafters as he strode toward a raised dais.

"Come, Aislinn."

She didn't tarry at Cameron's low command, her heart racing again when he drew her close against him as if protecting her from all of the curious glances, and proceeded to hustle her from the hall.

A strapping warrior and a long-limbed youth!

Yet something told her from the men's admiring looks—aye, and lustful, too—running up and down her body, word must have flown she wasn't a youth at all.

Muttering a curse, she decided as soon as she could, she would use her knife to crop her hair as close as it had been when she stowed aboard her father's ship.

"A good plan," Cameron muttered back at her, startling Aislinn that he'd read her mind until she realized her free hand had strayed to her short locks. "You're safer with me... unless the king intended tae lock you away in a tower. All these men, and few women save for servants—och, I may have tae fight our way out of here."

"I want twenty men tae accompany Laird Campbell," came King Robert's command from the dais, a loud scraping of benches upon the stone floor making Cameron curse this time as thrice that many rose to their feet. "You there... and you—and you! Follow them and make ready, they're leaving at once."

Suddenly it wasn't just Aislinn and Cameron leaving the great hall, but a host of boisterous Scotsmen striding after them.

"I dinna need more men, mine are enough," he groused under his breath, his arm tightening around her waist. He didn't stop hustling her until they were well into the central bailey, where he wheeled around to face King Robert's soldiers.

"Lady De Burgh is my intended bride and you will afford her all respect. Am I understood?"

At once, any appreciative glances vanished altogether at Cameron's menacing tone. To a man, the soldiers nodded and straightened their spines to stand at attention.

All of them stiffly awaiting his next command while Aislinn glanced up at Cameron to see an expression on his face that she had never beheld before.

Fearsome. His handsome features as if set in stone.

The formidable Highland warrior that King Robert had spoken of, suddenly right there beside her... his penetrating stare enough to make grown men falter.

So it seemed that several of the soldiers had begun to shake at the knees, but Cameron's roar to secure their weapons and horses sent them scattering to oblige him.

"Was that enough blustering for you?"

She met his eyes, incredulous that he could tease her after such a display, but it was the slow smile he gave her that made *her* knees suddenly feel weak.

Without another word, he kept his hand firmly at her back and guided her toward his own men who had already mounted their horses, while her spirited steed and his stallion snorted and pawed the ground as if eager to resume their journey.

It seemed within the blink of an eye, Cameron had lifted her up into the saddle as easily as if she were weightless, Aislinn feeling an intense wave of disappointment that they'd had no more time to speak to each other.

Her mind still reeled from his declaration to King Robert that he hoped to wed her—aye, Cameron had claimed her again as his intended bride only moments ago.

She had declared as well that she would accept Cameron as her husband with her father's permission, but what else was she to have said? If she had denied him, he might have refused to take her with him—ah, God, everything was happening so fast!

Did Cameron truly want her for his wife—or had that been the only way to convince King Robert to allow her to accompany him? So many questions and no time to answer them. And where was Cameron going now?

She watched, her heart pounding, as he strode toward a long, open-sided structure where a small army of blacksmiths labored, their hammers ringing out against anvils. She could see finished armaments hanging from hooks—spears, knives, aye, all manner of weapons—as Cameron ducked inside... only to emerge moments later with a sword that glinted in the sunlight and a round wooden shield.

His expression seemed unreadable as he came toward her, but again that slow, teasing smile spread across his face and made her heart seem to stop.

"Your sword, Lady De Burgh... compliments of King Robert. Lighter and shorter than my own, but deadly all the same. All I ask is that you dinna use it against me, will you swear it?"

"Aye, Cameron—*aye!*" She smiled, too, as she took the weapon from him, which made him stare at her face as if awestruck, but only for a fleeting moment.

She had no sooner thrust the sword into her belt, Cameron tying the shield with leather straps to her saddle, than he left her to mount his own horse.

His gaze never leaving her as his roared command resounded across the bailey for them to ride out from Dumbarton Castle.

CHAPTER 12

"Father, can you hear me? I just overheard the guards saying that we're leaving at dawn for Carlisle—*God help us, Papa*! Open your eyes if you can, I beg you."

William De Burgh felt as if he were swimming upward from a deep black loch, the pain so intense in his right shoulder that a fitful sleep was his only refuge. He stared at the anxious face hovering above his own and recognized Daran—but what had become of his handsome son?

Daran's skin looked ashen beneath a stubbly red beard, his blue eyes wild and stricken, his hair matted and filthy—aye, his clothing, too, and stinking like a cesspit—

"Father, they're going to kill us. MacGodfrey's assurances that we would be freed when the ransom comes were lies—*all lies*! We won't be here any longer but on our way to Carlisle and an executioner's axe, thanks to an edict just arrived from King Edward. We will never see our home in Éire again!"

Now William struggled mightily to rouse himself, though when Daran grabbed his tunic with both hands to shake him, he groaned in pain through cracked lips.

He had no strength any longer to scream, his eyes

filling with tears at the excruciating torment caused by any movement.

Stinging tears that blinded him as the babbling creature that was his beloved son crumpled into a heap beside the cot and broke into pitiful sobs.

God in heaven, why had his daughter Aislinn been born the stronger one? He had tried so hard to shape Daran into a man—a true warrior—but now he could see how miserably he had failed.

With the gravity of his son's words settling over him, William lifted his blurred gaze to the small barred opening in the door of their cell, which emitted the only light from the hall outside.

Emitted the only sounds, too, of the world beyond the dank walls of the dungeon, William wincing at the coarse laughter of the guards who must have heard Daran's weeping.

Ah, but could he blame his son? The bright prospect of fighting alongside King Robert the Bruce had been extinguished the moment they set foot upon Scottish soil... his kinsman Clive MacGodfrey betraying them.

That cowardly bastard hadn't even been a part of the attack, but had sent English soldiers posted at the stronghold to slaughter most of William's men and then take him, Daran, and those few still alive as prisoners. He hadn't known what transpired after being struck down on that rocky beach until he'd regained consciousness, to find a stoop-shouldered healer tending to his grievous wound while Clive hovered in the background—wringing his hands.

"I told them tae bring you here unharmed. Och, William, you fool! Could you not see that you were outnumbered and drop your sword? It's only the ransom we want—aye, myself and Earl Seoras MacDougall, my overlord—and not your life."

Such hatred had welled up within William at Clive's

treachery that for a moment he had forgotten his agony, his gaze falling upon Daran lying on an opposite cot and moaning.

"My son... *my son!*"

"Aye, at least he showed some sense and threw down his weapon—until he bolted for the ship and was cudgeled on the head. Och, dinna worry, he'll live... though you, William, I canna say for sure. A stronger blow and your arm would have been severed from your body, but my healer believes you'll heal if the wound doesna putrefy..."

Putrefy? William could smell the stench of his own rotting flesh and knew he was dying. All of the healer's poultices and potions had only prolonged his misery, and now this wretched news that they were bound for Carlisle at first light—saints help him, if there was only some way he could save his son.

Daran's anguished sobbing ringing in his ears, William had never felt more hopeless or more desperate, his mind racing.

Mayhap he could bargain somehow with Clive... promise him three times as much gold if he would secure Daran safe passage back to Ireland. If Clive would supply him with parchment and ink, he would pen a letter to his steward in Wexford just as he'd done two weeks ago when he had demanded their ransom be gathered and brought with all haste to MacGodfrey's stronghold.

Yet where was the gold? It should have taken Clive's men only three days to sail across the Irish Sea and deliver that letter, mayhap a few hours for his steward to secure the gold, and then a few days more for those same men to return to the stronghold situated along the Firth of Clyde.

Had something happened to them? A storm? Had they drowned?

If all had gone well, he and Daran and his remaining

men would have been released and sailing home before King Edward's accursed edict had arrived and changed everything. At least then William would have died upon Irish soil...

"Do not despair, son," he whispered, though his own tears wet his face and dribbled into his mouth.

Even if those men returned with the ransom, Clive would have to send the gold straightaway to Carlisle in compliance with the king's order. He had intended to keep it all for himself, since Earl Seoras had been slain little more than a week ago, while Clive had been allowed to leave the MacDougall fortress with his life.

He had gone there to report that a letter of ransom had been sent to Wexford, and had been invited to stay for a feast and witness the execution of some recently captured prisoners as the evening's entertainment—but unbeknownst to Seoras, Robert the Bruce himself had been among them. The feast Clive had anticipated had become a battle, with Seoras killed by one of his own warriors and the rescued king naming a new baron to the fortress, Laird Cameron Campbell.

A new baron that had shown mercy where William would have granted none, and permitted Seoras's courtiers that had survived the bloodbath to leave unharmed—Clive among them.

Clive had sat beside his cot and recounted the entire tale, rubbing his hands with glee at the thought of pocketing all the gold, while now he must be crying into his ale.

"Guards! I must speak with Laird MacGodfrey," William cried out as loudly as he could muster, though the effort cost him with a piercing stab of pain that stole his breath.

Would the promise of more gold arouse Clive's greed and get him to agree to a plan to save Daran? Aye, he might swear to it and then send out the letter across the Irish Sea and still do nothing to help them, but

William could pray, too, that Clive's conscience might be pricked now that he was dying...

"My son, come closer," William whispered to Daran, who had stilled his weeping to stare at him in surprise when he'd shouted for the guards. "Keep your voice low so they won't hear us. I have a plan that might save your life—"

"Only me, Father? What about you?"

William shook his head as Daran scrambled closer, his son appearing as nervous as a rabbit as he glanced at the cell door and back to him.

"I'll not live to see Carlisle, but you *must* live to take your place as the head of our family. The responsibilities will be great, and the first thing you must do is attend to Aislinn. You know that I arranged her betrothal, and she would have been wed before we sailed if Lord Butler hadn't been delayed by Wicklow rebels causing havoc on his lands. She wasn't happy about the match, the headstrong chit, but Lord Butler will be able to control her. A stern man, ten years older, with a firm hand—aye, that's exactly what your sister needs—"

"Papa, Aislinn's not in Wexford, but here in Scotland. I should have told you, but you've been so ill and I knew it would only distress you, forgive me!"

William stared in disbelief at Daran and tried to sit up, but he cried out in pain and fell back upon the cot, a terrible intuition gripping him.

"Mayhap she's dead, aye, I've feared it all along," Daran babbled on, clutching at his hand. "When I tried to run to the ship, she was there on the beach with Finnegan and a few others—her sword drawn though he held her back—"

"*A sword?*"

"Aye, I hardly recognized her with her hair cut so short—"

"*Her hair?*"

"Aye, like a man's, and she wore a tunic and trousers, but then I was struck upon the head..."

As Daran fell silent, rubbing the spot that still pained him, William felt such fury that he almost forgot his agony.

Aislinn had stowed away. God help him, was she somewhere in this dungeon? Her captors thinking her a youth if she was dressed like a man, for surely they wouldn't have considered her otherwise, with her slim build and long limbs.

Damn his daughter, what could she have been thinking? She was a young woman, not a warrior! She should have been safe at home and occupied with thoughts of a wedding and gowns to be made and a household to run when she became a wife, William's intuition making him lay the blame squarely at Finnegan's feet.

If his captain had stood beside Aislinn on the beach, then he must have known she was aboard ship and hadn't told him. Yet if Finnegan held her back, he must have known, too, that she would have been killed like so many others. Had Aislinn foolishly believed that she could wield a sword against seasoned soldiers? What madness had come to plague him during these final days of his life?

Groaning, William turned his face to the wall even as a key grated in the lock and a guard pushed open the door.

"William, you called for me? Daran, what has happened? Has your father grown worse? I'll send for the healer—"

"*No healer!*" His voice rasping to his ears, William turned back to face Clive, who wiped his mouth with a cloth as if he had just rushed from a meal.

Even with such news as he'd received about King Edward's edict, the man's gluttony never abated. As stout as a barrel, and standing no higher than Daran's shoulder, his son having jumped to his feet, Clive looked from him back to William.

"So we're bound for Carlisle and the executioner's block," he spat out, cursing the day he had allowed Clive to influence him to come to Scotland.

"Aye... and there's naught I can do, William. I was going tae come and tell you, but my supper was ready—"

"How many of my men are yet alive to accompany me and Daran in the morning? Six, seven?"

"Five now. Another died last night from his wounds."

"Is there a youth among them with bright red hair the color of my son's?"

Now Clive sputtered in confusion and glanced again at Daran. "Is his mind faltering? I can imagine it being so because of the pain."

"It's not his mind, Laird, but my sister he's thinking of. I just told him that I saw her near the ship on the day of the ambush... dressed as a man—"

"Your sister dressed as a man? I remember her from my visit tae Wexford, a bonny lass indeed. But there's no prisoner here with red hair like yours, and if a young woman had been among you, I would have been told, unless..."

As Clive fell silent, William tried to raise himself on the cot again, only to grimace and curse from the stabbing pain.

"My daughter, man! If she was there on the beach, she would have been captured along with my captain named Finnegan, who stood with her."

"Aye, but not brought here. A handful were taken tae Earl Seoras as proof of the ambush, just as I'd agreed. When I saw him the day before his death, he told me that Irish prisoners had been thrown into a pit and would rot there—"

"*Bastard*!" William lunged from the cot and grabbed

Clive by the throat before the man could squeal, though a white flash of pain caused his knees to buckle.

Together they crashed to the floor, William summoning every last ounce of his strength to throttle the life from the man who had caused them so much misery even as guards rushed into the cell.

It took three of them to pry William's death grip from around Clive's fleshy neck, the man coughing and sputtering and rolling away on the filthy floor to curse at him.

"Y-you attack me when I've done everything I could tae keep you alive? And now I'll have nothing tae show for it even if the ransom comes. Guards, *help me up!*"

With two men still restraining William, one of them digging his fingers cruelly into his wound, the third one assisted Clive to his feet while Daran huddled against the wall, sobbing again.

If his son had been a true warrior, he would have taken the chance to seize a sword and cut them all down, William thought bitterly, crying out in agony as the guards shoved him down onto the cot.

A weakling son and a reckless daughter. One most likely dead and the other soon to be, as Clive stormed from the cell without another word, dashing William's hopes of swaying him to send another letter of ransom to Wexford.

"I'm going to die... I'm going to die," intoned Daran brokenly, sliding down the wall to the floor and tucking his knees to his chest as he wept.

William said nothing, but closed his eyes to the disgrace that was his son and wished in vain that he'd had another moment more to strangle the life from Clive.

He had come so close to vengeance. *So close!*

CHAPTER 13

"Are you warm enough, Aislinn?"

Shivering in spite of the cloak she'd wrapped around herself, the night air grown so cool, she nonetheless nodded at Cameron.

What else could he do for her? No warming fire could be built that might signal their presence, his men hiding among the dense trees less than a league from the MacGodfrey stronghold.

Cameron had decided to stop here rather than further south alongside the road to Carlisle—and why continue on when they would discover soon enough if Irish prisoners were indeed held by her cousin Clive?

She had met that disgusting pig of a man only once at a supper in his honor when he had sailed to Wexford to meet with her father. She had watched in horrified fascination as Clive consumed enough roasted meat and trimmings for three men, but as soon as the talk turned to King Robert, she had been told to leave the room.

A fateful night filled with lies that had inspired her father to make ready to leave for Scotland and to turn his mind to her future, when for years he'd ignored her and left her alone.

That King Robert's imprisoned wife was also a cousin must have doubly swayed him, but whatever

Clive had claimed as to where his loyalty lay had sealed her father's resolve to cross the water—saints help her! Would she see him and her brother alive and breathing in the morning?

"Your teeth are chattering, Aislinn—here, come closer."

Already sitting near Cameron beneath a tree, she shivered again, but this time it wasn't because she was cold.

He had hardly spoken during their hours-long journey, Cameron a different man altogether when leading his men with his terse commands... though once again, he had bidden her to ride beside him.

Yet now, with their horses tethered nearby and resting in the darkness, an owl hooting overhead, it was her first opportunity to speak with him after what he'd said to King Robert—and what she had agreed to as well.

With a small sigh, she obliged him and scooted closer, Cameron's arm going around her shoulders to pull her close. At once she felt warmed by the heat of his body through his clothing, a blush firing her cheeks that she would even think of what lay beneath his own woolen cloak, and his tartan breacan and tunic.

Yet if they were to become husband and wife, was that so unseemly a musing? Let her not forget that Cameron had already seen her with no clothes at all—saints above! If holding her close could elicit such thoughts, what might happen if he went so far as to kiss—

"Did you get enough tae eat?"

Aislinn sucked in her breath and nodded, almost relieved that he had interrupted the stirring course of her imaginings.

Would the evening pass with nothing of any more significance discussed between them? If so, she would remain no closer to knowing if he had meant what was announced to King Robert. Just as he'd said, he hadn't yet broached the matter with her...

"Aislinn."

Now she froze, the husky timbre of his voice thrilling her as much as that he had drawn her even closer. She glanced with some embarrassment into the pitch dark. Were any of his men near enough to see them sitting so snugly together?

"I told them you were my intended bride... and it's none of their concern as tae how closely I hold you. Unless you're uncomfortable and I should move away?"

"No, no, I'm fine, truly," she blurted, astonished that Cameron had read her mind—and was speaking with little difficulty to her no matter she knew how hard he'd been trying to overcome his affliction.

Yet why wouldn't it be so? If she were indeed his intended bride, why would there not be an ease between them? A comfortable candor... though she didn't feel relaxed at all. The warmth of his breath tickled her ear and told her that his mouth was very close, if she only turned her head...

"I meant what I said today, Aislinn—"

"Ah, God!" Blurting out again, she felt chagrined to her toes that her thoughts could be read so easily, but his low laughter soothed her and made her feel all fluttery inside.

Never would she have imagined meeting a strapping Highland warrior like Cameron Campbell, his simple statement making her heartbeat race and her body to tremble. She didn't feel like herself at all, everything falling away—their reason for hiding in these pitch-black woods, her father, her brother, the danger they would face on the morrow—as his lips brushed against her ear.

"I want you, woman... and I will have you for my wife. Does that please you?"

She bobbed her head, for how could she not?

Cameron was everything a woman would want in a husband—handsome, courageous, kind, and yet fearsome if she was threatened. Her response seemed to please him, too, when he chuckled against her cheek.

"Will I hear you say that you want me as well, lass? You surprised me today when you spoke up so readily... and I hope it wasna because you feared the king would deny you accompanying me if you didna agree—"

"Aye, I admit that thought crossed my mind," she murmured in all honesty, his voice having grown somber. "You'd not said a word to me of your plan... t-to wed, I mean. I was as surprised as you—Cameron! Where are you going?"

He had released her and gotten up so suddenly that she wondered if he had heard a noise that concerned him from the direction of the road. Bereft of his warmth, she stared up at him, unable to see his face in the dark, and gasped when he pulled her up in front of him.

"Dinna trifle with my heart, Aislinn. I've never said those words before tae *any* woman, so if it wasna true that you would have me for your husband—"

"Cameron, how can you know so soon that you want me for your bride? You don't know much of me. I don't know much of you—"

"*I* know that I've never looked into a woman's eyes before without breaking into a sweat, but I could stare into your eyes forever. I've never been able tae speak with a woman before as I've done with you... never felt whole before... never had hope before..."

His voice breaking, he pulled her closer, his arms steely around her, while Aislinn wished so desperately that he could stare into her eyes now and see the truth shining there. She reached up and touched his face in the darkness, her fingers trembling.

"Aye, I want you for my husband... but my father is a hard man, cold and uncompromising. If we find him alive, I can only hope that he'll honor *my* choice... ah, Cameron!"

He'd embraced her tightly and lifted her from her feet, her arms flying around his neck as he found her mouth, his kiss possessing her.

His kiss consuming her as if something long fettered within him had broken free, Aislinn shaking from head to toe at the fierceness of it.

All she could do was hold on more tightly herself as he groaned her name against her lips. His hands slipped down to grip her bottom through her cloak and hoist her against him... though only for the briefest instant before he set her once more upon the ground.

Cameron shaking, too, his kiss no longer bruising but so achingly tender that she was certain her knees would give way beneath her.

"Aislinn... my Aislinn... "

His breathing as ragged as her own, she kissed him back as tenderly, though her heart had begun to ache.

She should tell him... aye, Cameron must know that she was already betrothed to another man so that she held nothing from him. Yet mayhap if her father and brother were no longer alive, it wouldn't matter and she would never have to speak of it—ah, God, forgive her for even considering such a thought!

"Cameron, you must listen to me," she pleaded against his lips, her heart hammering in her breast when he lifted his mouth from hers to look down at her. "My father... before he left—"

"Laird Campbell, look tae the north. *Fire!*"

Aislinn felt Cameron stiffen as the outcry from one of his men shattered the night's stillness. He thrust her away from him so abruptly that she gasped, though his hand upon her forearm kept her from falling.

"Stay here."

His tone brooking no argument, she nodded, but

already he had lunged out of the trees to the road where he had stationed a quarter of his men to stand guard.

She smelled it then, the acrid stench of smoke. She looked northward but could see nothing through the dense foliage other than a faint orange glow higher up as if from atop a hill.

Aye, Cameron had told her to stay, yet how else was she to know what was happening?

Biting her lower lip, Aislinn drew her cloak more tightly around her and followed his men that had abandoned their scattered hiding places to run toward the road.

Her face burned at the realization that some of them might have overheard her and Cameron, though he had said it was none of their concern. A brazen intended bride, aye, she could just imagine what they might have been thinking.

She was almost to the spot where he and his men had gathered, Cameron uttering a command for them to mount their horses, when her foot caught upon a root. She cried out, bracing herself for a fall, when she was swept up by powerful arms so abruptly that her teeth rattled.

"I thought King Robert told you tae do *exactly* as I say," he muttered fiercely, striding with her back into the woods. "God help me, Aislinn, this is no time tae defy me. The MacGodfrey stronghold is aflame, aye, which means an attack—else the English there decided themselves tae burn it."

"Aflame?" Aislinn echoed as Cameron hoisted her up onto her steed and then untied the tether. "My father, Cameron... my brother!"

He didn't answer, his grim silence chilling her as he handed her the reins. Then he untied his own horse and led their mounts by the bridle through the trees, most of his men already waiting for them out on the road.

"I would leave you here with guards if I thought you

wouldna ride off—by God, Aislinn, you promised the king that you'd stay close tae me. Mayhap he decided tae send some of his forces tae attack the stronghold after all, but we willna know until we're closer. Keep your sword at the ready!"

Her hand already gripping the hilt, Aislinn nodded and swallowed hard against tears that they might arrive too late.

Her father might have paid her no heed for much of her life, but she loved him all the same—aye, and Daran, always trying so hard to please him and yet never quite making the mark. What kind of justice would it be for them to have mayhap survived this far only to succumb to smoke and fire?

"Ride!" Cameron commanded, Aislinn urging her stallion into a gallop alongside his steed as his men came thundering behind them.

∼

"Hold!" Cameron pulled up on the reins just in time, a barrage of arrows raining down upon the road only twenty yards away as fire lit up the night sky.

From their position, he could see that the stronghold gates were aflame, as well as much of the front of a high palisade that surrounded a towering stone keep. A host of attackers with shields to protect them were shoving a battering ram against the burning gates, and already there was a gaping hole, the outer perimeter breached.

Yet who were those men? Clearly not English soldiers that he could see scurrying atop the part of the palisade that wasn't ablaze, their conical helmets glinting in the orange light and their raised voices filled with alarm.

Nor were they King Robert's forces for, to a man, they wore trousers beneath their tunics, so Cameron judged they weren't Scotsmen, either. The dark color of their clothing blended into the night and made it impossible for him to count how many were attacking the stronghold.

"Declare yourselves!"

Cameron cursed as another barrage of deadly arrows skewered the ground even closer to their position. He glanced at Aislinn, who stared in wide-eyed horror at the flaming gates.

Blast and damn! Why hadn't he stopped his men further back on the road where they could have dismounted and crept in closer, unseen?

"I said declare yourselves or die now—but if you're loyal to Edward, you'll die anyway!"

"Cameron, they're Irish," Aislinn blurted, holding tight to the reins as her stallion snorted and pawed the earth. "My father's kinsmen come to rescue him, surely."

Holding fast to his own reins, Cameron made a split decision and roared into the night. "Laird Cameron Campbell, and loyal tae King Robert the Bruce! We believe kinsmen of Lady De Burgh are imprisoned here."

No more arrows came after his pronouncement, the crackling of the flames growing fiercer and glowing red sparks flying high into the air.

So high that some of the wooden shutters at the windows of the tower had caught fire, a gasp coming from Aislinn.

Yet she screamed when the battering ram exploded through what was left of the gates, which startled her steed into a gallop, the reins tugged from her hands.

A gallop straight for the charred opening where Irishmen, roaring battle cries and brandishing their swords, pushed aside the battering ram and clambered inside.

"*Aislinn!*" Cameron could see she had lost all control

of her mount, and he spurred his horse after her, his
heart hammering.

He had never known fear in the face of danger, but
Cameron felt it now.

Not for himself but for the woman he loved, as her
horse jumped over smoldering debris and disappeared
into the bailey, the hem of her cloak catching fire.

Catching fire!

CHAPTER 14

A islinn clutched the stallion's dark mane and held on for dear life, dense smoke stinging her eyes—ah, God, was that her cloak on fire?

Neighing wildly, the stallion dug in his hooves and stopped so suddenly in the bailey filled with men fighting, men shouting, men dying, that Aislinn was pitched onto the ground.

She lay there for a moment, stunned, but then began to roll in the dirt to put out the flames even as an English soldier collapsed beside her—almost nose to nose.

Dead. His conical helmet split open and his lifeless hand still clutching a sword that had been meant for her, Cameron pulling her to her feet.

"Stay behind me."

She did, so startled—and grateful—he'd caught up with her and saved her life again, that her hand shook as she reached for her own sword, the wild melee of battle surging around them.

Yet no sooner was the gleaming weapon in her hand, but Cameron fended off another death blow as three English soldiers came at them all at once.

She would have died right there if not for the deadly

sweep of his sword that cut down their attackers like a scythe through harvest wheat.

Why had she ever thought she could fight like a warrior?

Aye, sparring with Finnegan had been one thing—but this terrible cacophony of death screams and the sickening sight of severed flesh and bone made her swear to herself that she would never entertain such foolhardy illusions again.

"Move over there behind those barrels, Aislinn!"

She scurried to obey Cameron's command, but then stopped as more English soldiers spilled from the entrance to the keep as if terrified rats trying to escape a burning ship.

Flames had sped up the walls from shutter to shutter to alight the wooden roof, which glowed against the night sky like a great flickering torch.

The Irishmen met their disoriented and outnumbered enemy head on, swords clashing upon shields as wounded and dying men fell to the ground in a heap.

Cameron grabbed her arm and tried to run with her to the barrels where they might have some cover—only for Aislinn to resist him as Clive MacGodfrey stumbled out of the keep, coughing from the dense smoke.

"Cameron, that's him—my cousin!"

Such fury filled her that she wrenched herself free and ran toward him, Aislinn pushing Clive with all her strength against the wall and pressing her sword to his throat.

"Where is my father? My brother? Tell me or I'll kill you this very moment!"

His pudgy face gone white, Clive stared at her as if seeing a ghost while Cameron rushed up behind her, his sword stained with fresh blood.

"By God, woman, *dinna run off like that again!*"

Aislinn couldn't say if the fearsome look on Cameron's face or her blade already piercing Clive's flesh swayed the man, but he gestured to the entrance he'd just escaped from as glowing sparks rained down upon them.

"The dungeon beneath the keep. Yet your father is near death—you canna save him!"

Such swamping relief had filled Aislinn, only to become horror at Clive's pronouncement, that she almost cut his throat. Only Cameron's strong hand covering her grip on the hilt stopped her, his voice low and urgent in her ear.

"We need him, Aislinn. Come."

Cameron grabbed Clive by his tunic and shoved him back inside the keep, the man starting to weep piteously.

"It wasna my idea! Earl Seoras demanded I deceive William for the ransom. He wanted more gold for his quest tae become King of Scots. Have mercy, Laird Campbell, just as you granted me a week past, I beg you!"

"Cease your babbling, man. The dungeon! Take us there or die right here."

Aislinn had never seen Cameron's face, sweaty and blood-splattered, look more chilling, Clive's sobbing instantly silenced as he bobbed his balding head.

With all of them coughing, the smoke growing thicker, she followed close behind Cameron as he shoved Clive ahead of them at sword point, the man leading them to the right until he stopped in front of a heavy oaken door.

"Through there, Laird."

So close to her father and brother, so close! Aislinn jumped when Cameron kicked open the door into what looked like a yawning pit of blackness, other than a sputtering candle in a wall sconce at the bottom of a flight of stone steps.

"How many guards are down there?" Cameron demanded, but Clive wildly shook his head.

"I dinna know—they might have fled."

"Pray, man, that one or two remain tae open the cells—aye, *pray*!"

Cameron went down the steps first, pulling Clive along with him, while Aislinn followed with her sword point now pressed against her cousin's back.

Thankfully there was little smoke, but she coughed all the same, feeling lightheaded of a sudden—she imagined from the painful swelling on the side of her head. So much for her skill with horses, but there was nothing to be done for the bump right now.

She glanced behind her at the sound of raised voices in the distance—aye, her father's kinsmen coming to find him!—and mayhap some of Cameron's men had joined in the search. Such gratitude filled her for whoever led the Irishmen, but she hadn't recognized anyone among those fighting so ferociously in the bailey.

A second flight of steps lit by another wall sconce and they finally reached the dungeon—the stench so thick of sweat, urine, and waste that Aislinn leaned against a dank wall for a moment to catch her breath.

"Aislinn?"

Cameron's voice filled with concern, she tried to give him a small smile, but truly, she felt like retching.

A dimly lit hallway went to the right and the left, with no guards in sight. Clive pointed to the nearest cell door where someone clutched the bars of a small opening—Aislinn gasping at the ashen face peering out.

"Daran!"

Hearing her cry his name, her brother began to laugh and weep at the same time as if half crazed, but how could it not be so after what he had suffered?

"The keys, MacGodfrey," demanded Cameron.

"T-the keys, aye, Laird." Whimpering again, Clive stuck his hand in a wall niche near the steps and then shook his head. "They're gone—och, the guards must have taken them!"

Cameron's vehement curse echoed up and down the hallway, while Daran's wild pleading made her heart sink.

"Aislinn, help us—*help us*! I don't want to die in this wretched place."

"Aislinn is here?"

A raspy voice drifting to them from inside the cell, Aislinn rushed to the opening and clutched her brother's hand, his fingers ice cold.

"Daran, Father is still alive!"

"Aye, sister—but I fear not for long. Saints protect us, am I dreaming?"

"No, no, it's not a dream," she tried to reassure him as she pressed her face to the bars. "Aye, Papa, it's me, Aislinn! We've come to get you out, but the keys are gone."

A terrible wail broke out from Daran, which made her spin around in desperation to see smoke curling down the steps like ghostly fingers. "Cameron, what are we to do?"

"Stand back."

She did at once, Cameron thrusting his shoulder against the cell door with such force that she heard the splintering of wood. Yet still the barrier held firm, though violent kicks from Cameron finally sent it crashing against the cell wall.

He rushed in first and Aislinn after, Daran collapsed upon the floor, weeping.

Her father lying upon a cot, groaning.

The sickening smell of rotting flesh making her stomach roil and now, Aislinn did double over and retch in a corner.

"Aislinn, help your brother."

She straightened and nodded, trying to fight off another wave of dizziness as she wiped her hand across her mouth and hastened to assist Daran to his feet. Cameron picked up her father from the cot, his scream of pain a terrible thing to hear. Yet what else could be done other than to carry him bodily out of the dungeon?

With Daran leaning heavily upon her, she followed Cameron from the cell, awestruck by his strength as her father was of sturdy build—only for them to meet a host of men spilling into the smoke-filled hallway.

"Save the other prisoners!" came Cameron's command, the harsh authority in his voice enough to spur them into action.

As several men rushed forward to help him carry her father up the steps, Aislinn felt overwhelming relief when two others flanked Daran and took him from her. She hastened after them while doors were kicked down behind her, freed men crying out with thankfulness as she coughed from the smoke.

Dear God, would there be time enough to save them all before the keep collapsed upon itself? Praying desperately, she stumbled up the last step only to be met by Cameron, who swept her up into his arms.

"My father?"

"The other two are taking him outside," was all he said, holding her close to shield her from swirling sparks that filled the air.

Her throat parched, her eyes watering, she buried her face against his chest and kept praying... for them, for the men she could hear emerging from the dungeon behind them—God in heaven, that the burning roof would hold for a while longer!

Aislinn couldn't have felt more relief when clearer air filled her lungs, telling her they had made it outside, too. Yet Cameron didn't stop until they had reached a palisade wall that hadn't been scorched, where many were gathered well away from the flames.

He didn't release her, but hugged her fiercely while Aislinn wound her arms around his neck to hug him back. She could feel his heartbeat pounding against her breast, his breathing ragged, but they were safe.

A few moments more and she finally looked around her while Cameron still held her close, her father lying upon the ground not far from them, while Daran knelt beside him.

At once she grew tense, fearing the worst, but she exhaled with relief that her father still lived, when he lifted his head and looked at her.

His drawn face illuminated by the flames as, with a great whoosh, the roof caved in and fell with a thunderous crash into the keep.

A startled outcry went up, Aislinn glad to see that more men had joined them at the wall. Some were hunched over and coughing while others, huddled upon the ground, appeared to be rescued prisoners. Thank God, *thank God*!

Even Clive MacGodfrey had been hauled up from the dungeon and was slumped against a barrel, noisily sobbing again.

"My father, Cameron—I must go to him."

With what seemed great reluctance, he hugged her again tightly before he set her down, and then clasped her hand in his.

Together they walked to where her father lay, while another man—as sturdily built but taller—stepped forward as well.

At once the Irishmen standing nearby bowed their heads in deference, the stern-looking man clearly their commander—though Aislinn had no idea who he might be. His gaze falling to her hand in Cameron's and back to her face, she felt a sudden chill that he looked so... furious.

"Papa," she murmured, drawing closer, though she saw no affection in her father's eyes, only harsh disapproval as he looked her up and down.

"You're not a man, but a woman," he grated, even

speaking making him grimace in pain. "Your hair... your clothing. You shame me, Aislinn... *shame* me and your family."

Tears sprang to her eyes as everyone seemed to be looking at them, his harsh words not what she had expected at all. She glanced at Cameron, who squeezed her hand as if to reassure her though his expression had hardened.

"Lord De Burgh, your daughter deserves your thanks for helping tae save your life and not your rebuke—"

"Take your hand from her, Laird Campbell!" demanded the Irish commander, who came closer.

He appeared ready to draw the sword sheathed in his belt while Aislinn felt Cameron stiffen beside her, though he didn't reach for his own weapon. Instead he glanced at her, something chilling her in his darkened eyes, while she stared back at him in confusion.

"Do you know this man, Aislinn?"

"No, I've never seen him before—"

"He's your betrothed, Lord Aengus Butler," her father cut her off, clenching his teeth as he raised himself on one elbow, while Daran looked up at her with pity. "You would have known him quite well as your wedded husband if you hadn't stowed aboard my ship and now disgraced us all."

Aislinn heard Cameron suck in his breath, but he didn't move, as if rooted to the ground.

Aengus Butler. Aye, her father had told her the man's name as the one he intended for her to marry, but she had never met him!

She didn't know what to say, what to do, the world suddenly crashing in around her as surely as had the flaming roof.

Her temples throbbed, her heartbeat thundering in her ears. She looked from her father, who had fallen back onto the ground, groaning, to Lord Butler, who

MY HIGHLAND PROTECTOR

glared at both her and Cameron, and then up into the
dark sky as her knees wobbled beneath her.

A terrible pain shooting through her head, ah, God,
was she dying?

The last thing she saw was Cameron's face above
her, his stricken voice calling her name as if from a
great distance... and then cold, numbing oblivion enveloped her and Aislinn heard no more.

CHAPTER 15

"God help you, Campbell, the woman's betrothed! Her pledged husband as powerful a man in Éire as you are here, if not more so. Did Lady De Burgh not say a word of it tae you?"

Cameron shook his head at King Robert, who sighed heavily and continued his pacing.

"Och, you've known her for hardly a week, it canna be so great a loss. A wife will be found for you, your clan will see tae that soon enough."

Like another blow to the gut, Cameron said nothing, but held his silence as the king went to the window to look out in the direction of the River Clyde.

"Where *is* Lord Butler? His warship lies at anchor and I see commotion aboard, but no rowboat being lowered. He demanded this meeting upon his arrival in the wee hours of the morning, as if I dinna have other matters on my mind—like Edward preparing for battle near Carlisle. A rumor flies that he's not well, but I doubt that will stop him from ordering his forces north tae try and defeat me—aye, let him come."

Instead of turning around to face him, King Robert seemed to fume at the window while Cameron stood at attention in the king's personal chamber—the future he'd envisioned with Aislinn nothing but ashes.

The moment she had collapsed last night, Aengus Butler had rushed forward and pushed him away from her while William De Burgh had cursed him for allowing his daughter to accompany him into danger.

Cursed him!

Cameron's clothing covered with burn holes from the sparks and his hair singed—och, but none of that had mattered at the ashen pallor of Aislinn's face. Only then had he seen the egg-shaped lump on the left side of her forehead, an injury she must have suffered when she was pitched from her horse.

He hadn't been close enough to save her from falling, and had jumped from his own horse when she was rolling upon the ground to put out the flames at the hem of her cloak. Everything after that had been a blur of fighting to keep them both alive, and the desperate rescue of her father and brother—och, and then the terrible realization that she had lied to him in not revealing her betrothal.

Lied to him!

Cameron's gut clenching, he wanted only to leave Dumbarton Castle and return at once to the fortress and leave this entire debacle behind him.

He and his men had arrived before dawn after an exhausting ride from what was left of the MacGodfrey stronghold to see that Lord Butler's ship was anchored beyond the shallows, the water route proving much swifter.

Cameron had reported at once to the castle, and had been met by one of King Robert's captains and told to get some rest and come back later that morning.

The king had already been apprised about everything that had happened by Lord Butler, and Aislinn and her father and brother and the other freed prisoners had been taken to the castle infirmary along with the Irishmen wounded in the battle.

At least his own men and those of the king hadn't

suffered grievous injury, a few of them sent to the infirmary. Cameron found himself wondering, in spite of his resolve to thrust Aislinn and her deception forever from his mind, if she fared better that morning.

How could he not? He loved her still though he felt as if his heart had been ripped from his chest, yet what did it matter?

She was soon to wed another man, something Aislinn had known before she stowed away, Cameron cursing the moment she had set foot upon Scottish soil.

"She'll need complete rest and quiet—my chief healer told me as much right before you arrived," came King Robert's voice to wrest Cameron from the bitter tumult of his thoughts. "You said she fell from her horse and hurt her head, Campbell?"

"Aye."

"Pity. Such an injury can be deadly, I've seen it happen many a time. One moment you appear well enough, and then you're not—och, but she canna stay here. Nor can Lord Butler return tae Éire with her in such a precarious state. I want her taken tae the Carmelite convent not far from Dumbarton, the same one where Lady MacLachlan pretended she was mad. Who knows if the poor lass will ever leave it?"

Cameron swallowed hard, this news only making him more anxious to be on his way back to Campbell Castle.

He could do naught for her. Even if he could, Lord Butler would never allow him anywhere near her. He would never see her again... never look into her eyes... never speak tae her...

"Mayhap he's changed his mind about the meeting." King Robert turned from the window to look intently at Cameron. "I assured him that you're an honorable man, Campbell, and wouldna have done anything tae compromise the lass before marriage."

"So he knows I wished tae wed her?" Cameron bit off, the king nodding.

"Aye. He wasna pleased. He's a harsh one, but that's none of my concern. Since she's my wife's cousin, I'm duty bound tae see that she's well cared for until she recovers... *if* she recovers."

King Robert's last words cutting into him, Cameron muttered, "Aye, harsh like her father," as a sharp rap came at the door, making him stiffen.

"Enter."

Cameron didn't have to turn around at the king's command to know it was Lord Aengus Butler who strode into the room, the air suddenly charged with tension.

"King Robert. *Laird Campbell.*"

His name spat out, Cameron slowly exhaled and told himself to remain calm.

He had come too close to raising his sword last night when the man had shoved him away from Aislinn. Soon this unwanted audience would be behind him and he'd be on his way back to the fortress... without her.

"Do you care tae sit, Lord Butler?"

"No, I'll stand."

Again King Robert heaved a sigh, Cameron guessing that he wasn't so keen for the meeting, either. "Very well. Say what's plaguing you, man."

"Aye, I will! You assured me upon my arrival that this Highlander is an honorable man—"

"A *baron*, Lord Butler," King Robert cut in, "and entrusted with one of my most formidable fortresses because of his courage and loyalty. He saved *my* life nine days past, aye, he and his brother Conall and his former commander, Earl MacLachlan, and they have my abiding respect and gratitude. Is that enough of a commendation for you?"

Sputtering under his breath, Aengus glared at Cameron. "Aye, your words hold great weight, my lord king, but I'll have your baron speak for himself and tell me if he's had his way with my betrothed. From the look of it last night when he carried her from the stronghold—"

"The roof was ablaze!" Cameron shot back at him, clenching his fists. "Only moments from collapsing. What was I tae do? Leave her tae fend for herself in the hope that she'd make it out alive through the smoke and flames? I swore tae her father's man, Finnegan, when he lay dying that I'd protect her—"

"Aye, Finnegan, that bastard! Lord De Burgh told me last night while we made our way here that his *trusted* captain must have known Aislinn had stowed away, but neglected to inform him. His son saw Finnegan standing beside Aislinn right before Daran was struck upon the head—"

"How is William's son?" King Robert interrupted as if to diffuse some of the mounting tension, shooting a look of caution at Cameron.

"A disappointment to his father, but he'll mend in time. Why is it that strong men are cursed with weak sons? *Mine* will not be weak, I can assure you. I'll plow my new bride good and hard to ensure the sturdiest seed takes root—"

"By God, man, are you a rutting beast tae speak so of Aislinn?"

"Lord Campbell, *hold*!"

King Robert's command the only thing that kept Cameron from drawing his sword, his knuckles white as he gripped the hilt, he saw that Aengus had grasped his weapon as well.

"Answer his query and let's have done with this meeting," commanded the king in a harsh voice, glaring at Cameron. "Did you have your way with the lass?"

"I kissed her."

"Anything else?"

"I embraced her."

"And?"

"I told her I wanted her for my wife and she answered that she chose me for her husband."

"*Chose?*" Aengus spat with derision. "No woman chooses whom to wed. Her father promised her to *me*, and we would have been married before William left for Scotland if my lands hadn't been attacked by Irish rebels. As soon as the insurgence was defeated, I went to Wexford to claim her as I'd told her father I would do in a message sent to him right before he sailed—and Aislinn was gone! It wasn't until the letter of ransom arrived from Clive MacGodfrey the same day that I suspected she might have stowed away—aye, William warned me that she's outspoken and headstrong. Yet I can see those as desired attributes for begetting strong sons, wouldn't you say, Campbell?"

Cameron knew that Aengus was goading him into wielding his weapon, his stomach churning that the man would speak of Aislinn as if she were no more than a vessel for breeding.

She was strong and beautiful and brave and bold—and mayhap dying, God help him. What could he do? Lie to the man that he had lain with Aislinn and already claimed her?

If she recovered from her injury, mayhap she didn't want him after all and had lied to him so that he would take her to her father.

A man as cold and hard as the one standing within a sword's stroke away... daring him still with a gloating look in his eyes that he had won without Cameron having to utter a word.

"I did not lie with her, my king."

"Enough, then, we're done here. Leave us, Campbell, and I will speak tae Lord Butler, and then with Lord De Burgh, about having Aislinn transported tae the convent—"

"A convent?" blurted Aengus. "I plan to sail tomorrow with my betrothed and her father, who barely clings to life, as well as her brother and as many of my men that can stand—"

"Can *she* stand, Lord Butler?" King Robert demanded in a low, tight voice. "Have you seen her this morning as tae her condition?"

"Aye, she's not yet opened her eyes or spoken, but Lord De Burgh wishes to die upon Irish soil. I will return in a month's time with more men to fight with you against King Edward."

"I'm grateful that you would join our battle for freedom from English tyranny like many of your countrymen, but my wife's cousin will not be traveling anywhere other than a quiet place where she may recover... if it is God's will that she lives. Leave if you must tae honor her father's dying wish—"

"I will not leave without her."

"Then you'll be staying in Scotland for a while longer. As for Lady De Burgh's father, he came here tae fight as well, so our soil is as good as any other for a grave, aye, Lord Butler?"

Sputtering again, Aengus glanced from King Robert to Cameron, his expression hardening. "You will not see her."

"Aye, Lord Campbell is forbidden tae see her," came the king's answer for him. "He'll be riding north within the hour."

Cameron swallowed against the fury that threatened to choke him, not at King Robert, to whom he nodded in deference.

One lunge and he would have Lord Butler by the throat, the smug look wiped from his face. Aislinn could have told him a hundred lies—a thousand lies—and still Cameron ached to see her one last time...

"Leave us now, Cameron."

His gaze shot back to King Robert, who had never

called him by his given name before. Did he see sympathy in the man's eyes, even pity?

"Aye, my lord king."

Cameron didn't nod nor give any look of acknowledgment to Aengus as he strode from the room, his fury not abated moments later when he stepped outside.

The bailey was filled with men and noise and commotion, aye, no fit place at all for Aislinn to recover... *if it is God's will that she lives.*

King Robert's words flying back to make him curse aloud, Cameron stormed toward where two of his men awaited him with his horse.

His massive stallion tossed his head at the sight of him, his glossy black coat marred by tiny red marks where sparks had scorched him. It was the same for Aislinn's steed held outside the towering walls where the rest of his men were gathered for the ride back to Campbell Castle—God help him, her horse no longer.

Had her father demanded last night with what remained of his strength that her knife and sword be cast into the Firth of Clyde to sink into the dark depths?

Had she been stripped of her tunic and trousers and the cloth binding her breasts—if she lived, never to wear men's garb again? Oddly enough, it had suited her... though to see her in a silk gown with her red hair once more long and flowing had been a fervent dream —och, never to come true. Blast and damn, why was he tormenting himself?

"Laird Campbell!"

Ready to mount, Cameron turned around to see Daran De Burgh hobbling toward him with the help of a wooden crutch thrust under his left arm.

The young man looked pitiful—nearly eighteen, Aislinn had told him, his shoulders hunched and his face gaunt and pale from the torment he'd suffered, though he wore clean clothes and his hair, as red as hers, had been washed. It occurred to Cameron that

Aislinn's male garb must have been some of her brother's. The young man extended his thin hand.

"I want to thank you... for saving my life. It should have been said by my father as well..." His voice faltering, Daran looked even more downtrodden at the mere mention of the man, and he jumped when Cameron clasped his cold fingers with firmness.

"I, too, had a harsh father. He kicked me and my younger brother, Conall, out into the world as lads, but we made our way as best we could—serving one overlord after another, learning tae fight, tae survive." Cameron released his hand and looked him straight in the eye. "You will survive, too, once your father is dead. Yet only you can decide if he'll have beaten you and marred your life forever—or you will emerge stronger and determined tae face whatever lies ahead. *Stand up tall, Lord De Burgh!*"

Cameron's roared command not only made Daran jump again, but drop his crutch to the ground.

"I-I'm not Lord De Burgh—"

"You will be soon enough. Did you hear me or do I need tae shout louder?"

Daran looked as if he didn't know what to do, though he straightened his shoulders and raised his chin.

A spark of something suddenly alight in his blue eyes—och, the color so similar to Aislinn's, Cameron couldn't help thinking, making his heart ache.

"Do you need that crutch?" he demanded sternly, finding it impossible to thrust Aislinn from his mind.

"Only to help me walk, Laird. I still feel so weak."

"Yet you came forward tae thank me, aye? I see no weakness here, only strength, for in doing so, you've defied your father and set your own course. Am I not right?"

Nodding as if Cameron's words were sinking in,

Daran appeared to gain several inches right in front of him—the young man standing much taller.

Cameron didn't say anything more, but turned back to his horse and mounted, his men following suit.

That Daran had come from the infirmary where Aislinn lay with her eyes closed, not speaking, mayhap hardly breathing, while he had been forbidden to see her—

"She's called your name, Laird, my sister. If she wakes, is there anything you want me to tell her?"

His hands clenching the reins, Cameron cursed himself for having delayed his leaving to speak to Daran —for he could have gone the rest of his life without knowing that Aislinn had cried out for him.

Aye, it would have been better.

"Wish her happiness in her marriage," Cameron said bitterly, wheeling his horse around and heading toward the castle gate.

CHAPTER 16

"Sweet child, will you not open your eyes? It's a fine morning, and the sisters and I thought you might enjoy a walk in the courtyard after you've had some breakfast."

Aislinn heard Sister Agnes's voice well enough, the older woman sitting beside her bed, but she kept her eyes closed and feigned sleep, which made the nun sigh.

"I know you're awake, Aislinn, and I dinna fault you for not wishing tae appear so. Remember how I told you that I had another lass here, Magdalene, who didna want tae leave the convent? She had no choice when her husband, Laird Gabriel MacLachlan, came tae fetch her, but they found happiness together and I pray you will, too."

"I will never be happy if I'm wed to Lord Butler, Reverend Mother," Aislinn said barely above a whisper, opening her eyes to look into the nun's kind face. "I would rather you had let me die."

"Och, now, child, let's have no such talk." Sister Agnes crossed herself and, as if for good measure, she lifted the gold crucifix hanging by a chain around her neck and kissed it before letting it dangle once more. "We feared, indeed, that you might not survive the injury tae your head, but a week of rest and much prayer have wrought a miracle—"

"Not a miracle, Reverend Mother, if I must marry a man I cannot love!" Tears stung Aislinn's eyes as she buried her face in her pillow and began to weep while Sister Agnes clucked her tongue with dismay.

"Cannot love? Surely you will find contentment tae have a home and protection, aye, and when your sweet bairns come, you'll have love enough then tae fill your heart—ah, child, please dinna cry."

How could she not cry? Aislinn felt like she'd awoken to a nightmare ever since she had found herself lying in an overcrowded infirmary that reeked of sweat and urine, her brother sitting beside her cot and holding her hand.

Her head pounding fiercely, her vision blurred, she had been too weak and dizzy to lift her head while Daran had told her what had happened—her collapse at the MacGodfrey stronghold, her transport aboard Lord Butler's ship to Dumbarton Castle, and that she would soon be taken by oxcart to a convent not far from town, where nuns would care for her.

King Robert's orders.

Ah, God, at least for that she could be thankful, for what her brother had told her after had filled her with despair.

"Cameron..." she had murmured feebly, her heart sinking when Daran shook his head.

"He's gone, Aislinn, an hour past. I spoke to him before he left—"

"Did he know I was here?"

"Aye, but he was forbidden to see you."

"No, no, surely that cannot be. Surely he said something to you—"

"Only to wish you happiness in your marriage to Lord Butler..."

Her marriage... her marriage... her marriage!

Aislinn cried out and squeezed her eyes shut as if she could stop the words from echoing in her mind— while Sister Agnes looked at her with growing concern.

"Ease yourself, child, I beg you. Lord Butler willna be pleased if you suffer a setback—God help us, you know he's coming here later today tae fetch you! What will he say when he sees your face swollen from weeping?"

"I care nothing for what he thinks and I will not marry him! I love another, Reverend Mother, I've told you as much. Laird Cameron Campbell. What will I do? *What will I do?*"

Aislinn had never been one for weeping, but now it seemed she could not stop while Sister Agnes rose from the bed and began to pace the small room, her long black habit swirling.

Magdalene's former room in the nuns' sleeping quarters, making Aislinn think again of the spirited young woman who'd had no say over whom she married —*no say!*

Yet their stories were different for Magdalene had already been wed by proxy when Laird MacLachlan had come to fetch her, while thankfully, Aislinn was still unmarried.

Magdalene's feigned lunacy had brought her here— aye, Sister Agnes had shared some of her wild antics, chuckling even—while Aislinn had been more dead than alive when she had been carried by Lord Butler into this room and laid upon the bed.

Swamping dizziness and a numbing sleep had claimed her again after what Daran had told her, Aislinn's heart aching so badly that she had craved oblivion.

She remembered nothing of the journey by oxcart to the convent. Yet Lord Butler had shaken her roughly awake as Sister Agnes and the two other nuns who had cared for her so diligently over the past week, Sister Hestia and Sister Tabitha, had gasped in horror.

Lord Butler's face contorted with fury, his voice low and ominous.

"You will be my bride, Lady De Burgh, whether Laird Campbell has lain with you or not! He claimed he only kissed and embraced you, but I don't believe him —yet no matter. I want strong sons—*not* weaklings like your pitiful brother—and seed growing inside your belly will accomplish my aim whether it's that Highlander's or mine. Do you hear me?"

Aye, Aislinn had heard him through the haze enveloping her and the piercing pain in her head, making her cry out when he pushed her back down upon the bed—and the nuns to gasp again.

"Don't think your father's death will alter anything, for Daran has sworn to uphold Lord De Burgh's wishes. Tend to her well, Reverend Mother. I'll send a messenger to bring me a report every day. *Every day!*"

At the stark memory, Aislinn wept all the harder while Sister Agnes continued to pace with a vigor belying her threescore years, until a rap came at the door.

Aislinn fell silent at once, hiccoughing, and Sister Agnes rushed to let Sister Tabitha into the room, the plump nun's usually cheerful face marred by distress.

"God help us, Lord Butler is already here?" blurted Sister Agnes, but Sister Tabitha shook her head.

"No, Reverend Mother, but a messenger has come from Dumbarton Castle. Forgive me, Lady De Burgh, for bringing you such grievous news. Your father has died, God rest him."

Aislinn could but stare at her, stunned that he had survived so long, though Daran had told her, too, that King Robert's chief healer had believed he might be able to save him.

She hadn't been able to glance to the right or left at the infirmary for the fierce throbbing in her head, but she had heard her father's agonized cries as the rotted flesh was burned with a red-hot iron from his shoulder —no, no, no, she didn't want to think of it.

Nor her father's cruel words about her shaming him and disgracing their family, instead of offering thanks to Cameron—or her—for saving his life.

Everything she had done to try and make him see her differently had been folly!

How could she have hoped that he would change his mind and allow her to choose her own husband one day?

The man Aislinn loved as surely as she breathed... yet Cameron must hate her now for not telling him the truth about her betrothal.

Tears tumbling again down her cheeks, Aislinn turned her face to the narrow, mullioned window and the brilliant morning outside that seemed to mock her sorrow.

Not for her father, though she prayed that he had found peace, but for Cameron, whom she would never see again, while Lord Aengus Butler would soon arrive to claim her—

"Enough tears, Aislinn, you must get up! I'm certain your betrothed will be coming here all the sooner tae fetch you for your father's burial."

She stared in shock at Sister Agnes, who gestured for Sister Tabitha to leave the room and then threw aside the covers.

Her stern tone unlike anything Aislinn had heard from so caring and good-hearted a woman, though Sister Agnes's hands were gentle as she assisted her out of the bed.

A sudden wave of dizziness made Aislinn stagger a bit, that ill effect from her injury still not having left her, but Sister Agnes held onto her arm until Aislinn gave her a small nod.

"Good, now you must get dressed. I'll fetch your clothes."

As Sister Agnes went to a plain wooden chest at the foot of the bed and threw back the lid, Aislinn felt a terrible certainty that all of her desperate entreaties had fallen onto deaf ears.

She couldn't have been more astonished when the nun didn't retrieve the sapphire-colored gown Lord Butler had sent over yesterday, but a neatly folded pile of clothing, and a leather belt and pair of shoes that Aislinn at once recognized.

"Here, you must hurry if you're tae put some distance between yourself and Lord Butler. At least with your tunic and trousers, you'll look more a youth and less worthy of notice."

"Reverend Mother!" Her heart racing, Aislinn stripped out of her nightgown and wound the binding around her breasts, Sister Agnes tying the cloth at her back.

A few moments more and she was fully dressed, the nun handing her the same fur-trimmed cloak that had caught fire but with the hem now mended.

"It's warm today, but the nights are cool. I canna let you out the front gate in case others might see you, but you're a brave and clever lass. I know you'll find a way out of the convent. Your escape must come as an utter surprise tae me—do you understand, Aislinn?"

She bobbed her head, such gratitude filling her that she couldn't speak as Sister Agnes moved to the door. Yet the nun turned around suddenly, her eyes shining with tears, to look at Aislinn.

"Mayhap you think because of my sacred calling that matters of the heart are a mystery tae me. I sought refuge here years ago because my husband was slain by English soldiers. I loved him so—a good and honorable man like Cameron Campbell. I know that about him from what you've told me—all he's done tae help you, and because I saw it in his face when he came here with Laird MacLachlan tae fetch Magdalene."

"You've met him?" Aislinn blurted, reaching out to squeeze Sister Agnes's hand.

"We did not speak, but enough now, Aislinn. I canna say what God holds in store for you, but I pray it's not as the wife of Lord Butler. Ride straight tae the north and by dusk tomorrow, you'll come upon Campbell Castle—"

"*Ride*, Reverend Mother?"

"Aye, there's a farm close by where you'll find ponies grazing in the pasture. I know the man well, he's a generous patron of our order. Tell him I need one of them, which is true enough—*for you*, sweet child. God bless and keep you."

Sister Agnes stepped forward to wrap Aislinn in her arms with the kindest hug she had ever known, and then the nun released her to open the door and disappear out into the hall.

Leaving Aislinn so stunned still, that she didn't move for a long moment as her gaze swept the room.

Her refuge, too—ah, God, would Cameron open the gates for her if she was able to find her way back to his fortress?

And even if he did, wouldn't Aengus know to seek her there and demand her return?

So many unsettling questions swirled in her mind, but now wasn't the time to worry about what might happen—but to flee!

Aislinn ran to the door and after a quick glance, she ducked into the empty hallway. She heard low murmurings from other rooms, the nuns at their morning prayers, which made her whisper one, too, that she would quickly find a way out of the convent.

She tried not to make a sound as she hastened outside, closing the door to the nuns' quarters as quietly as she could. The stone walls around the convent were high, but not so much that she couldn't climb over them if she found some way...

Her breath caught at the sight of a covered rain barrel resting against a nearby wall, Aislinn struck by a surge of hope that her desperate prayer had been answered.

Wasn't that a sign from heaven that all would be well? She kept right on praying as she climbed atop the barrel, biting her lip at the dizziness that assailed her, and jumped upward.

Her hands caught the top of the wall. With all the strength she could muster, she hoisted herself up and over and jumped down this time, exhaling with a whoosh when she hit the grassy ground hard.

She didn't wait to catch her breath, but set off at a run for a copse of trees where she could find cover. Only when her back was up against a gnarled trunk did it occur to her that she hadn't asked Sister Agnes where the farm lay from the convent. North? To the west?

Closing her eyes, her heart hammering, she murmured another prayer, a low nickering carrying to her on the breeze that stirred her hair.

She glanced to the east, relief swamping her to see a sod-covered farmhouse and a pasture beyond it where shaggy ponies were grazing on lush grass—aye, *ponies*!

Aislinn swallowed against a flicker of pain across her head and bolted for the farm even as she heard the thundering of hooves in the distance.

Her heart in her throat, she didn't have to glance behind her to know that Aengus and some of his men were approaching the convent—God help her, how would she ever outride them on a pony?

Aislinn didn't stop until she was almost to the pasture, but slowed her pace so she wouldn't startle the creatures. She glanced at the farmhouse, though no one was in sight. A thin curl of white smoke rose from a hole in the roof that carried a whiff of porridge bubbling, mayhap the family gathered for breakfast.

Her own stomach growling, she prayed for forgiveness as she crept toward the nearest pony.

She had no time to seek out the farmer and ask for his help as the pounding of hooves and whinnying of horses grew louder. Even if she did, speaking to him would only point to Sister Agnes—no, no, the last thing she wanted was for that dear woman to suffer for helping her to escape.

"There now... easy..." She held her breath as the sturdy animal turned its head to look at her with deep brown eyes—all the while Aislinn praying he wouldn't bolt. Still moving with great care, she grasped his thick mane and pulled herself onto his back.

She had no saddle, no bridle, no reins, only her years of loving and caring for horses to guide her as she urged the pony into a trot away from the commotion near the convent.

The trot soon becoming a gallop as Aislinn steered the animal north with her heels while she clutched the pony's coarse mane more tightly.

Dumbarton behind her and the purplish hues of the Highland mountains in front of her... only for Aislinn to veer moments later to the northeast as she sensed with cold certainty that Campbell Castle was exactly where Aengus would think she was headed.

Tears filling her eyes that she would find her way instead to the small farm where she and Cameron and his men had spent the night... hot porridge covered in fresh cream and fresh baked bread awaiting them before dawn.

CHAPTER 17

"By God, Cameron, will you train us tae death? The men need some rest—I need some rest."

Cameron scowled at Conall, who had thrust his sword into the dirt so he could wipe the sweat from his face. "They'll train until *I* say it's time tae stop, brother. Will the whole lot of you grow soft and when King Robert calls upon us tae fight, we willna be ready?"

"We'll be ready, but mayhap half dead at this pace. You've been back for over a week and every day since, we've been up at dawn and training well past dark—like tonight!" Conall lowered his voice and came closer, scowling himself. "I'm truly sorry for the heartache you've suffered, Cameron. Aislinn was as bonny and brave a lass as any man could hope for, but you didna know she was betrothed and she didna tell you. I asked her, too, and would have warned you—"

"So she lied tae both of us, what does that tell you? We were both fooled, but it doesna matter anymore. She's wed by now."

"Aye, or in her grave because of falling from her horse and striking her head. *No* man claiming her, neither you nor Lord Butler—"

"Enough, Conall, pick up your sword!" Clenching

151

his teeth at the thought of Aislinn dead, Cameron swung his own sword before his brother was ready, Conall jumping out of the way just in time.

Blast and damn, he wasn't working his men any harder than he was working himself—anything tae keep his mind from flying to Aislinn, always Aislinn!

Something told him that she wasn't dead or he would have known it in his heart—aye, felt it in his bones, too. Yet she was dead to him all the same, for if she had recovered at the convent—as he had been praying with more fervor than he'd ever prayed before—then she would be married to Aengus Butler by now and lost to him forever...

Cameron drew a deep ragged breath and swung at Conall again, that thought almost too grim for him to bear.

The ring of sword clashing against sword echoed around the bailey lit by great, sputtering torches as a hundred men went at each other, thrusting, parrying, ducking, and even tumbling into the dirt to escape a blow... until at last, Cameron roared out for everyone to stop.

Aye, *roared*.

He smiled to himself in spite of the terrible ache in his heart at the memory of Aislinn teasing him—God help him. He would have given everything for more time with her... more teasing, more talking together, more embracing, more kissing, the sweet softness of her lips something he would never forget.

"Aye, I believe you did love her..." murmured Conall in amazement, followed by a low whistle that made Cameron sober at once and wipe the sweaty grime from his face with his sleeve.

"I love her still... though it will bring me nothing—och, release the men tae their supper and their beds."

As Conall obliged him, his brother's shouted command sounding so much like his own, Cameron sheathed his sword and walked wearily toward the keep.

He hoped Uncle Torence wasn't awaiting him in the great hall. The man had arrived today with news of more hopeful brides—a half dozen of them, which made Cameron sigh heavily as he glanced up at the bright half-moon.

More than enough light, along with the torches, for training this late—but Conall was right.

Cameron had been pushing his men too hard. Himself too hard. Yet how else was he to get any sleep at night if he wasn't so exhausted that all he did was collapse into bed without even stripping off his clothes?

He didn't want to think, to dream, to wish in futility, or to pray in vain that by some miracle, he and Aislinn might still be together.

He had spoken of her lies to Conall, but in his heart, he didn't fault her for them. Who could say what had made her keep such a thing from Conall? From him!

Cameron had known her only a few days after all. Hardly enough time to share such intimate details of one's life with each other... though he had asked her pointedly if she was wed or betrothed. How could so beautiful and rare a lass as Aislinn De Burgh not have been promised in marriage?

"Tae such a man as Aengus Butler," Cameron muttered bitterly to himself as he stepped inside the keep.

Harsh, uncompromising, vulgar, and much older... the thought of him touching Aislinn disgusted Cameron, though he could not thrust the image out of his head.

From what she had said outside the MacGodfrey stronghold, she hadn't even met the man, though she must have heard about him from her father.

Had his plan for her marriage caused her to stow away on his ship in a desperate attempt to show him that she had a mind of her own? That she was strong and courageous and could fight—though it had all gone so horribly wrong.

All I ask for is a say over my own life...

Aislinn's words haunting him, it was suddenly so clear to Cameron that she hadn't lied to him at all. Why speak of her betrothal when she clearly hadn't accepted it? She had chosen *him* for her husband, not Lord Butler —och, why was he tormenting himself? The thing was done, never to be undone—

"Cameron, come and join me for a cup of ale!"

Cursing under his breath at his uncle's shouted invitation, Cameron reluctantly turned back toward the great hall.

The massive room was dark except for a smoldering glow in the fireplace, though Uncle Torence wasn't alone. A pretty serving maid stood nearby holding a pitcher, ready to fill his cup as soon as he emptied it, while he brandished one in his other hand as Cameron approached him.

"Aye, we've much tae celebrate! You have eight lasses vying for your attention now—and all of them bonny. Isna it grand?"

The man was drunk, that was plain, Cameron determined to drain the brimming cup in one swallow and retire to his bedchamber where he would attempt to sleep.

"Sit, nephew, sit."

"I'll stand, Uncle Torence."

"What? You've no time tae visit with me when I've come all this way again with a message from our chieftain? He wasna happy that you sent those two poor lasses away and that you made a spectacle of yourself with that young Irishwoman."

"A spectacle?" Bristling, Cameron took the cup from him, more so to keep his uncle from spilling the stuff all over himself as he leaned forward in his chair.

"Aye, I heard the whole thing... you swearing tae

take her tae King Robert and embroiling yourself in her affairs. A good riddance tae her in her trousers and boots, no shame in that one at all. You, meanwhile, were staring at her like a besotted fool—aye, I saw it! Conall joined me for a cup himself while you were still training your men and told me Lady De Burgh is tae wed another, if she lives. A pity, her injury, I'll grant you that... "

As his uncle paused to take a long draught of ale, Cameron, frowning, set his own cup down upon a trestle table.

He hadn't seen Conall slip away, but his brother was as quick on his feet to steal away for some ale as he was with wooing women.

"You're not going tae drink with me?" demanded Uncle Torence, beckoning for the serving maid to refill his cup. "You must know, Cameron, that our chieftain has spoken of petitioning King Robert and demanding that you wed one of these lasses straightaway tae strengthen your position—"

"You mean the clan's position," Cameron said tightly. "I would think the Campbells pleased enough tae have me as baron here instead of still bowing and scraping tae the likes of Earl Seoras MacDougall."

"Aye, they're pleased, nephew, but you must have sons. *Sons*! How else will you hold onto this fortress and your lands?"

"By my loyalty and service tae the king—and *whomever* I wed and *whenever* I choose tae do so, I might very well have only daughters!"

Now his uncle did spill ale down the front of his tunic as he gasped in dismay, his broad face grown bright red. "Och, man, dinna say such a thing. Cross yourself now and say a prayer, you didna mean it!"

Cameron gave a grim laugh and not only didn't cross himself, but left his uncle staring after him as he strode from the hall.

Their entire exchange not only infuriating him that his clan would pressure him to marry—but a wave of such poignant understanding gripping him as his thoughts jumped once again to Aislinn.

He had a choice as to whom he might wed, no matter what his uncle had said about their chieftain.

Yet she had *no* choice! By God, if he ever was blessed with daughters, Cameron swore then and there never to make them suffer as Aislinn might be suffering right now at Lord Butler's hands—

"Cameron!"

He didn't stop no matter Conall came striding after him, and he cursed aloud when his brother caught his arm.

"A messenger has come from King Robert. He demands—with regret—that you return Aislinn at once tae Dumbarton and Lord Butler if she has made her way here—"

"Made her way here? What are you saying? Aislinn's not here—*is she?*" Now it was Cameron who grabbed his brother by the tunic, his mind racing that such a thing might have been kept from him for whatever reason—yet his heart sank when Conall shook his head.

"No, I would have told you, Cameron. The messenger said that Lord Butler had gone tae the convent two days ago tae fetch Aislinn for her father's burial—but she wasna there. The nuns in an uproar that she could have escaped without anyone seeing her—"

"Aislinn... escaped." Such elation gripped Cameron that she was alive—*alive!*—and yet anguish, too.

Where was she? Two days ago... surely she would have found her way to the fortress by now, for where else would she have gone? Unless she had gotten lost or something terrible had happened to her...

"Dinna invite trouble, Cameron," Conall's voice broke into his tormented thoughts as if reading his mind. "Aislinn's a clever lass. She would remember the way and know well enough tae hide if she sensed danger."

"Aye, she's clever," Cameron echoed, meeting his brother's eyes. "Did the messenger say anything else?"

"Only that Lord Butler and his men searched around the convent in all directions, but they didna find her. The other thing amiss was that a pony had been taken from a farmer's pasture."

"A pony. So she's riding..." Cameron could not say why, but this news made him chuckle to himself, Conall looking at him as if he had gone mad.

"Canna you see?" Cameron quickly sought to reassure him. "She has her wits about her, brother—her injury not plaguing her so much that she didna know what tae do. But if she's not here, then where...?"

Conall appeared at a loss, shaking his head, though Cameron felt a sudden niggling of hope that his clever, beautiful, and brave Aislinn might have thought of somewhere else to take refuge.

Mayhap at first she had considered riding north to Campbell Castle, but surely she realized that Lord Butler would have guessed her plan.

"King Robert gives you three days tae bring her back, Cameron, or he'll send some of his men with Lord Butler tae fetch her. It's a wonder he hasna done so already instead of the messenger bringing us this news."

"With King Edward in Carlisle, he willna spare any of his forces unless he must—"

"But she's not here. None of this is making any sense... unless you've some idea of where she might be..."

A long, low whistle escaped Conall before Cameron could say a word about what his gut intuition was telling him, and already he was striding to the entranceway.

"Cameron, do you think she went tae that farm you

told me about—where you spent a night after saving the girl from those English soldiers?"

He spun on his heel to face Conall, who had followed close behind him and stopped short, staring back at him.

"Keep it down, man." Cameron jerked his head toward the great hall. "Uncle Torence will hear you—though he's probably too drunk tae remember a thing."

"Och, he's sleeping in his chair by now," Conall replied with a shrug. "That's what you're thinking, aye? You said the place was a few hours' ride from Dumbarton and a league off the main route, so even if Lord Butler came north without King Robert's men, he would never know tae look there—"

"Dinna speak of this tae anyone," Cameron cut him off as he stepped outside with Conall again following him. The bailey was empty except for guards on patrol, and he shot over his shoulder, "Where's the messenger?"

"I already sent him tae the barracks—the man was exhausted."

"Good. I'm leaving you in command just as before."

"Leaving me in command?"

"Aye. I'm riding out tonight, alone. It will be faster that way. I canna wait a moment longer."

Cameron heard Conall's sharp intake of breath, but it would be easier for him as well to hide along the way if the need arose; not so, if he were accompanied by twenty men like the last time he had ridden south toward Dumbarton.

"Send the messenger out at first light with an answer for King Robert that Aislinn isna here, which is the truth—at least for now."

This time a low curse came from Conall as his brother caught up with him just before he reached the stable.

"You're bringing her back?"

"Mayhap here, mayhap further north, I dinna know where we'll go—but I swear that Aengus Butler will *never* have her, not as long as I breathe."

"Are you mad, Cameron? Aye, I hoped Aislinn might be the one for you, but that was before we knew of her betrothal. Her finding her way on her own is one thing —but for you tae lay claim tae her now? You know such a move will bring both the King of Scots and an irate Irish lord down upon you. You'll lose everything, this fortress, your title!"

Cameron wheeled around so abruptly that Conall fell back, startled.

"What do I care for those trappings if Aislinn isna by my side? You'll never understand because you've never loved *any* woman, just dallied with them and se-duced them—aye, and broken more than a few hearts along the way! It's a pitiful life you've led, Conall, not tae care for another soul more than your own cravings and desires."

Cameron could see at once that Conall's expression had darkened, but the harsh words were said and couldn't be withdrawn—not that he would do so.

His brother needed to hear them, for who knew what might happen once Cameron defied King Robert? Conall might soon find himself named the new baron of Campbell Castle with their clansmen hounding *him* to take a bride!

At that thought, Cameron gave a dry laugh, but he felt no humor.

Aislinn was out there somewhere—mayhap in a warm bed with a roof over her head and food in her stomach and kind people surrounding her... or mayhap not.

That latter possibility made him lunge into the sta-ble, his pressing thought to saddle his stallion and head out into the night.

He was hungry, aye, but he didn't want food.

He was exhausted, but he didn't want sleep.

To see Aislinn again... aye, to hold her in his arms and know that she was safe, was *all* that he wanted.

This fortress and his brother's reservations and a king's displeasure be damned.

CHAPTER 18

"S he smiles at us, Mama, but still she looks so sad."

Aislinn found it hard to swallow her mouthful of porridge at Sorcha's half-whispered comment to her mother, but it was true all the same. These good people, Leith and Jeanne MacLean, and their sweet daughter, had offered up their home the moment Aislinn appeared on their doorstep two days ago, and had given her food and shelter.

As they finished their breakfast in companionable silence, Leith, a strong, sturdy farmer, got up from the table and went outside to resume his morning chores while Jeanne began to clear away the bowls.

"Let me help you," Aislinn offered, but the kind-faced woman shook her head.

"You need more rest, go on back tae bed with you. You're no longer pale as when you first came here, but all the same, I'd feel better about it."

"Oh, Mama, Aislinn promised she would help me gather the eggs this morning."

"Indeed, I did... I'll be fine, truly." Aislinn rose from the table and went to a peg near the door where she had hung her cloak, and settled the garment around her shoulders. "I'll be nice and warm against the morning dew. Shall we go, Sorcha?"

The beautiful girl bobbed her head, Aislinn thankfully seeing no ill effects after the terror Sorcha had suffered at the hands of those English soldiers. As blond, blue-eyed, and fair as her parents were both dark-haired and brown-eyed, Sorcha grabbed Aislinn's hand once they were outside, as if to hurry her along.

She couldn't help wondering again at the difference in looks between parents and daughter, but she supposed such an odd thing could happen when it came to children.

She remembered Cameron, too, had appeared surprised when Leith and Jeanne had run from their home to tearfully embrace Sorcha, their love for the girl so evident in the kisses and hugs they had rained down upon her.

Was it two weeks already since that happy reunion? Then, later that evening, Cameron had given Aislinn his own knife so she would have a weapon to protect herself—ah, God, it hurt so much to think of him.

Was he thinking of her, too? Or had he thrust her forever from his mind, believing that she had married Aengus Butler? Mayhap he thought her dead... or mayhap he hadn't thought of her at all for not telling him about her betrothal, and only believed the worst of her—

"Aislinn, why do you look so sad? Are you thinking of Laird Campbell?"

She nodded at Sorcha, her heart warmed by the girl's compassion, for she had told the family the truth of why she had fled to their farm.

How could she not when her presence here might cause them danger? She prayed constantly that Aengus wouldn't find her... her greatest fear that he might somehow make them pay for harboring her. That terrible thought made it hard to force a smile as they reached the chicken coop on the far side of the barn.

"I've forgotten most of their names," she said as

lightly as she could muster, grateful for her cloak on this cool, cloudy day. "Hmm, but I think Speckles is the dark brown rooster with white spots—"

"You love him, aye, Aislinn?"

"Who? Speckles?"

Sorcha's bright, infectious laughter made her laugh softly, too.

"No, Laird Campbell!"

Aislinn sobered, her heart aching again, though she nodded. "Aye, I love him."

She had never said the words aloud before—and what good would they do her? Yet Sorcha clapped her hands together as if she couldn't be more pleased, and then pointed excitedly beyond Aislinn's shoulder.

"Good, then you must tell him."

"Tell him?"

As Sorcha giggled and kept pointing, Aislinn felt as if she were rooted to the ground, no more able to turn around than she could dare to believe that Cameron—

"By God, woman, will you not greet me?"

She spun around, the sudden movement making her feel dizzy even as Cameron reached out to pull her into his arms.

Strong, muscular arms as she stared with utter amazement at his handsome face, her eyes filling with tears.

"*Cameron*... how?"

"A fortunate guess, is all... but you're here, Aislinn. Thank God, you're here."

She saw then the fatigue at the corner of his eyes, though he chuckled as Sorcha skipped around them and then ran off to the front of the barn, calling her father.

"She's a good set of lungs," he murmured, stroking the hair from the side of Aislinn's face as she still stared at him, hardly believing her eyes.

"You... you don't hate me?" Aislinn had whispered the words, terrified for a moment that Cameron might disappear like a phantom and she was dreaming, but he pulled her closer. His embrace so warm, so wondrous—aye, flesh and blood!

"Hate you?" Tenderly, he kissed her at the spot where she had struck her head. "I feared you must hate *me* for leaving you... for not coming tae your side even tae say goodbye."

"Daran told me you were forbidden to see me... and that you wished me happiness—"

"Dinna say it, Aislinn, for you'll not be marrying anyone but me... if you want it. Only if you want it..."

Such joy flooded her, all the sadness and misery and heartache of the last days swept away as she threw her arms around his neck. "Aye, Cameron, I want to marry you. Yet how can that be? I'm still betrothed to Lord Butler—*oh!*"

Cameron's mouth silenced her in so impassioned a kiss, his arms lifting her from the ground, that she forgot all else but the wonder and warmth of his lips pressed against hers.

She sensed then as surely as he held her, kissed her... that he had claimed her for his own—*saints in heaven, she prayed that it would be so!*

A dizzying moment later, Aislinn felt her feet touch the ground when she heard fresh giggles from Sorcha and someone gruffly clearing his throat.

Cameron's arms fell from around Aislinn, but he found her hand and clasped it as they both turned to face Leith MacLean.

"Laird Campbell, I'm glad tae see you. My wife and I have been wondering how long it might take you tae find her—Lady De Burgh, I mean... but we knew you'd come."

"So did I!" piped up Sorcha, glancing from her father to Aislinn. "Did you tell him that you love him?"

Cameron's hand gripping hers all the more tightly, Aislinn felt her face afire as she looked up to find him staring at her with an intensity that made her knees feel weak.

"Not yet... I... we—"

"Och, child, let's leave them alone," broke in Leith, glancing at Jeanne, who stood near the house with a broad smile on her face as she wiped her floured hands in her apron. "I'm sure they've much tae talk about without us troubling them—"

"Oh, but Papa!"

Sorcha kept up her protests all the way to the house, where Jeanne gave her a big hug and then shepherded the girl inside, followed by Leith.

Only then did Cameron once again pull Aislinn into his arms, his gaze filled with teasing as he stared into her eyes.

"Hmm... did I hear the lass say that mayhap you loved me?"

"Mayhap?" Aislinn teased him back, though she shivered at the way he looked at her... Cameron sobering now as his blue eyes darkened. "I think she sounded fairly certain of it."

"Och, woman, I'll not know for certain until I hear you say the words—but mayhap you want tae hear them first from me, since it's you that cured me."

"Cured you?" she whispered, not only shivering as he nodded, but her heartbeat thundering.

"Aye, Aislinn. You've made me whole—och, as whole as can be until you're fully my wife. I love you and *no one* will keep us apart, I swear it! They'll have tae slay me—"

"No, no, don't say such a thing," she cried out, pressing her fingers to his lips. "I would die then, too, for I wouldn't want to go on without you. I love you, Cameron..."

She fell silent, her heart aching with such love for him that her throat had grown tight, tears again springing to her eyes.

One trickled down her cheek and he bent his head

to kiss it away, and then lifted her chin and pressed his mouth to hers—Aislinn tasting the salt upon his lips.

A tremor from deep within rocking her that they yet faced such uncertainty no matter what they wanted so fiercely... ah, God, let her not think of that harsh reality right now.

She felt Cameron grow tense, too, as if struck by the same thought that their path ahead was a precarious one. Yet why couldn't they pretend even for a short while that nothing stood in the way of their happiness —*nothing*!

A low nickering carried to Aislinn as Cameron, with great reluctance, released her and turned to where his stallion walked toward them.

The reins dragging upon the ground, the massive animal appeared as exhausted as Cameron, whose face was lined with weariness in the sunlight that broke through the heavy clouds.

"Och, I didna tether him. I saw you and jumped down, not thinking..."

His voice tinged with the same weariness, Aislinn felt a rush of concern. "Did you ride through the night?"

"Aye, except for a few stops tae rest him—but dinna worry, love." Cameron drew her into his arms again and kissed her cheek. "Seeing you again and knowing you're safe is all I needed tae revive myself—"

"Yet you're exhausted, I can see it," Aislinn cut in gently, though his nuzzling at her ear thrilled her as much as hearing him call her *love*. "You must get some sleep—if only for a few hours. The day is young, Cameron, surely there is time for you to lie down for a while..."

She grew silent at his expression darkening, his embrace around her tightening, too.

"Do you know how I learned you ran away from the convent? A message from King Robert, and he's given me three days tae return you tae Dumbarton or he'll send some of his men with Lord Butler tae come after you."

"So they thought I'd gone to Campbell Castle just as I feared," Aislinn murmured. "That's why I came here, and I prayed and hoped that you'd know where to find me... if you wanted to find me. I wasn't certain after I didn't tell you about the betrothal—"

"All of that's behind us now," Cameron said with such finality that she couldn't help but feel reassured. "I realized that you didna reveal the truth because you never accepted your father's plans for you—and you'd hoped so fervently tae sway him and make your own choice."

"Aye, Cameron, *you*! You're my choice—ah, God, I still can't believe you're here and we're together. Who could have known that stowing aboard my father's ship would bring me to you? If only I could have moved his heart—"

"You moved mine, Aislinn"—Cameron pressed his lips briefly to hers—"and mayhap one other. It didna strike me until I was on my way here that the messenger said something about regret by King Robert."

"Regret?" Aislinn echoed as Cameron nodded, staring into her eyes.

"He knows I love you. Wanted tae wed you—aye, *will* wed you... which is why I believe the king didna allow Lord Butler tae ride north the same day you ran away from the convent. How that must have enraged him. He's proven himself tae King Robert as not only a harsh man, but a brutal one—and you're his wife's cousin. I'm certain that weighed upon his mind—and his heart—when he sent a messenger tae tell me you'd fled and gave me three days tae bring you back tae Dumbarton. Three precious days."

Now Cameron kissed her so fervently that Aislinn

sighed against his lips, but still her mind raced with confusion.

"Cameron, I-I don't understand," she admitted, feeling breathless when he raised his head to stare at her again. "Three days?"

"Aye, Aislinn... for he knew where I'd find you because of our English prisoner. We told the king about what happened on the way tae Dumbarton, remember? When we went tae ask him if he would allow you tae accompany me tae the MacGodfrey stronghold?"

She sucked in her breath, nodding and feeling so foolish for having forgotten they had bared so much to the king. Mayhap her memory had suffered because of her injury; either that or she had been so preoccupied with thinking about Cameron. Heaven help them, they weren't safe here after all!

"Dinna fear, love. I'm certain King Robert has said nothing about our whereabouts tae Lord Butler, and that English soldier is locked away deep in the castle dungeon. The king gave us three precious days so I could find you and claim you as my bride—och, God only knows what will come after, but for now, we must find a priest."

She shivered at the huskiness in Cameron's voice and the stirring import behind his words. Yet a cold chill suddenly struck her at the thought of what Lord Butler had vowed while Sister Agnes and the two other nuns had looked on with dismay...

"Aislinn?"

She had grown stiff in Cameron's arms, shaking her head. "He'll not rest... Aengus. He told me that he would have me for *his* bride whether you had lain with me or not—so our marriage will not dissuade him. If he doesna go so far as to try and kill you, he'll demand an annulment—ah, Cameron. What are we to do?"

Tears welling in her eyes, she didn't feel strong and

courageous at all, but on the precipice of losing the man she loved!

"Look at me."

She did, trembling as Cameron lifted her chin, his gaze intense upon her.

"We're not tae fear what may come tomorrow. I would never have gone into battle if I'd allowed such thoughts tae plague me... and we're in a battle now. *No one* is going tae take you from me... the woman I love. Say you believe me, Aislinn."

"Aye, I believe you."

"We're going tae fight whatever comes... you and I... side by side. Have you ever imagined a more fearsome pair? You... like a Norse shield-maiden, a valiant woman warrior, aye, that's what you appeared tae me the day you stole my sword."

"And you?"

"Your husband and protector... proud and grateful tae stand beside you. Rest will come later, Aislinn. For now, let's find ourselves a priest."

CHAPTER 19

"I fear for my brother, Gabriel. He's not thinking like a warrior, but a besotted fool! If Cameron lays claim tae Aislinn and defies King Robert, he'll lose everything. I tried tae tell him..." Conall fell silent as his former commander and longtime friend seemed to ponder his words while Magdalene stood beside him, clasping his hand.

The tawny-haired beauty, as petite as Gabriel was tall, appeared thoughtful, too, and glanced from her husband to Conall.

"He must love her very much tae risk all that he's gained. I will pray that we'll have a chance tae meet Aislinn soon."

Meet her? Was Gabriel's new wife as blind as his brother to the consequences of disobeying their king? Certain now that his headlong ride to MacLachlan Castle had been for naught, Conall sighed heavily and looked down at his dusty boots.

He felt beaten and disheartened—as much that Cameron wasn't thinking at all rationally as that the two of them had exchanged heated words.

Well, it had been Cameron, actually, to flail Conall up and down for his dalliances with women—yet he had never heard a complaint from one of them.

Aye, mayhap some of them had broached the possibility of marriage with a satiated whisper here and a fluttering of eyelashes there, but that had always been his cue to hastily retreat by whatever means offered the least resistance. Now that he thought of it, there had been one or two that had blocked a doorway to keep him from leaving and he'd had to climb out a window—

"You find some humor in your brother's predicament?"

Conall sobered at once and met Gabriel's eyes. "Not at all. We had strong words before he left the fortress... quite disagreeable, really, though it led me just now tae think of something else—och, forgive me. What do you suggest we do? Wait here for word that Cameron has been thrown into the dungeon at Dumbarton Castle? If that happens, the king might appoint a new baron tae take his place, mayhap even myself, and then Clan Campbell will be coming after *me* tae take a bride—by God, man, think of something!"

Now it was Gabriel that laughed, Magdalene smiling, too—for surely she knew as much as her husband that marrying anyone was the last thing Conall wanted to do.

Yet they both grew serious again; Cameron riding out into the night in desperate hope of finding Aislinn was indeed a weighty matter.

"Gabriel, we must ride straightaway tae Dumbarton and make an appeal tae the king that he allow Cameron and Aislinn tae wed."

Conall looked with surprise at Magdalene, but she was looking at Gabriel as if the decision had already been settled upon.

"*We?*"

"Aye, husband, I'll not stay here pacing up and down and wondering what's happening. Dinna forget that Aislinn is cousin tae the king's wife. Do you think he would truly allow Lord Butler tae take her back tae Éire after what he must know about him? Conall, didna you just tell us that Cameron said the man possessed a harsh temperament?"

"Aye."

"Uncompromising... brutal, even?"

"Aye, that as well."

"Och, it reminds me of what happened tae my sister, Debora..."

Conall swallowed hard at the tears suddenly glistening in Magdalene's eyes, and Gabriel drew his wife close to comfort her.

Conall remembered her sister, too, from his days as a young guard at what had been the MacDougall fortress... Debora so lovely and sweet and kindhearted, but none of that had saved her from an arranged marriage to a cruel man.

Six months later and the poor lass was laid in her grave—her untimely death affecting everyone who had known her, especially Magdalene. She had spent four years in a convent feigning lunacy to spare herself the same fate, but thank God, Gabriel was as good and honorable a man as Cameron...

Conall exhaled heavily, feeling disgusted with himself now.

What would it have cost him to wish his brother well instead of railing at him about losing lands and title —things that he and Cameron had never thought to possess?

They had fought together for one overlord or another in countless battles... splattered with blood and muck... and yet in this battle of the heart, Conall had failed him!

If the plan Magdalene had proposed might grant Cameron the chance to wed the woman he loved, aye, the woman who had cured him of his lifelong affliction —och, who was Conall to stand in the way of his brother's happiness?

"I agree with your lady, Gabriel. King Robert gave Cameron three days before he'll order any move against him, and today's the first of them. Even if we leave by midday, we willna arrive in Dumbarton until tomorrow afternoon. I told you that I have an idea where my brother went tae find Aislinn, though not the exact place, so we'd have tae search for them—"

"We've no time tae waste. No, we'll go directly tae King Robert and make our appeal—and my clever wife will accompany us."

Conall remembered that commanding tone in Gabriel's voice from when he'd served as one of his trusted captains, and knew that the final decision had been made.

As Magdalene threw her arms around Gabriel and stood on tiptoe to kiss him, Conall found himself wondering what it must feel like to have earned such devotion—*och, whatever was the matter with him?*

Love caused nothing but torment and trouble. Look at what Gabriel had gone through with Magdalene... and now Cameron with Aislinn, and the outcome was yet unclear!

"I'll leave Alun in charge here while we're gone— and Finlay will ride tae Campbell Castle with your order allowing him tae assume command until you return. Is that acceptable tae you, Conall?"

"Aye." Glad to have something else to think about than love and devotion and the sheer madness of it all, Conall had no doubt that Gabriel's captains, Finlay and Alun, would capably handle such responsibility.

They were former brothers-in-arms, after all.

United again in a common purpose for Cameron— God help them that their appeal didn't arrive too late.

～

"My wife."

"My husband." Aislinn's whisper following Cameron's as the old priest intoned a blessing and made the sign of the Cross, she could barely focus upon the words for the wild beating of her heart.

They were married, truly bound together. Astonished by the brevity of the ceremony, she stared into Cameron's eyes and he, into hers... her trembling hand held so firmly by his as the priest gestured for them to follow him.

Another man in brown clerical garb, their only witness, walked quietly ahead to a low table where he sat down while the priest shuffled to one side.

"Our church record," explained the friar, dipping his pen into a small bowl of ink. "Cameron Alexander Campbell."

"Aye."

Aislinn shivered at the resonant sound of Cameron's voice and the scratching of pen upon parchment as his name was written into the leather-bound book.

"Aislinn Eleanor Campbell... formerly De Burgh."

"Aye," she murmured, Cameron still holding her hand and gently squeezing her fingers.

More scratching came and then the friar blew upon the ink; Aislinn jumped a moment later when he closed the book with a thud and rose from the table.

"Godspeed tae you both."

"Aye, Godspeed," echoed the priest with a last disapproving glance at her trousers.

She had feared at first he wouldn't perform the ceremony because of her garb, though much of it was covered with her cloak, but Cameron had told him that they were travelers and had no other clothing for her to wear—aye, the truth.

Except for the delicate white nightgown embroidered with wildflowers, which Jeanne had pulled from a chest she was filling for Sorcha's marriage one day, Aislinn's eyes welling at her kindness.

"For your wedding night," the woman had murmured, giving her a hug. "You'll look so lovely for him."

Now, Aislinn trembled anew as Jeanne's words echoed in her mind, the priest and their one witness disappearing like wraiths through a side door.

For your wedding night...

Yet it wasn't night yet, only midday, Cameron leading her into the narthex of the small stone church, where he swept her into his arms.

"I must kiss you."

He did, Aislinn gasping at his embrace in a holy place, but cradling his face all the same and kissing him back.

"Our own blessing for this day," Cameron whispered when he lifted his head, though still he nuzzled her ear. Then he seemed to shudder and he released her so abruptly that Aislinn gasped again, his fingers entwining with hers to lead her outside into what had become a balmy summer day.

The heavy clouds gone, no threat of rain. The air smelled sweet with wildflowers that made her think once more of the nightgown wrapped in a piece of linen and stuffed into a bag hanging from the saddle, Cameron's horse tethered to a post.

Upon seeing them, the black stallion whinnied and bobbed his head as if congratulating them upon their marriage, which made Aislinn giggle.

Only to fall silent when she saw Cameron staring at her as if he couldn't believe his ears. It dawned on her that he'd not heard her laugh much at all since they had met just over two tumultuous weeks ago—ah, God, how could so much have happened to them in so short a time? They were husband and wife now!

"Dinna stop," he said to her, staring at her face, but the moment had passed. Yet that didn't keep her from smiling at him with wonder, Cameron truly the most handsome man she had ever seen.

The light breeze stirring his hair as black as his stallion's, the masculine beauty of his features holding her spellbound.

"We're not yet at the inn tae look at me so, wife," he said with a husky voice that thrilled her, though she felt a sudden rush of nervousness.

Cameron was a big man, so powerfully built, and while no one would think her petite, she still felt much smaller beside him. Was all of him so... so—

"There you go again," he murmured, his hands encircling her waist to lift her up onto his horse. "Enough of that now, woman, or we'll shame ourselves in the street."

Aislinn blushed to her roots, not so much from what he had said, though she guessed well its meaning, but that she'd never before seen such a look upon his face.

Hungry. His expression tense, as if the very act of touching her had aroused something carnal within him.

She wasn't so ignorant of what occurred between a man and a woman upon marriage—or otherwise—to not know what lay ahead, but she was a virgin. If Cameron had been so sorely afflicted with shyness since boyhood, might she find him untried as well? Was such a thing even possible for a warrior of such strength and power?

Aislinn felt as if her face was afire as Cameron looked at her with such intensity that she guessed he must have read her thoughts—saints help her!

His blue eyes darkened to a turbulent hue.

His hand clenching the reins as he didn't join her in the saddle, but led his stallion toward a cluster of cottages and sundry buildings further down the road from the church.

She sensed his answer without him saying a word, her nervousness flaring again at what would soon ignite between them when he had been so long denied.

She had felt his tension during their shared ride together, too, though she'd offered to take the pony for the short journey, her bottom wedged between his muscular thighs...

Aislinn drew a shaky breath, remembering the last time that had happened, when Cameron's closeness had made her tremble.

In a hopeless effort to distract herself, she focused upon the good-sized village where Leith and Jeanne had sent them, which lay four leagues from their farm... the inn ahead owned by her uncle, Broden MacHugh.

Cameron had never said he'd left the fortress in such haste that he had no coin with him, but when he had asked if they might return to the farm after their wedding and sleep in the loft of the barn, Jeanne had been aghast.

"You'll do no such thing, Laird. My uncle owns a comfortable inn, not an unruly drinking place at all. Tell him I said tae offer you their best room and we'll settle with him later—our gift tae you. And now you'll eat something while Leith brushes down and feeds that fine horse of yours. I can imagine you're in a great hurry tae wed, but love willna calm an empty belly!"

With that, Jeanne had laid out a fine meal for him, eggs fried in butter and sizzling slices of salt-cured pork and fresh baked oatcakes—and Cameron hadn't refused her.

Aislinn had eaten more, too, at Jeanne's insistence, the woman's whispered advice of, "You'll need your strength, lass, with such a strapping Highlander as that one," making her blush now all over again as Cameron drew the stallion to a halt outside the Rose and Thistle Inn.

"Wait for me, Aislinn."

She nodded, wondering how long it might take him to explain to Jeanne's uncle about the MacLeans' generous gift... only for Cameron to reappear mere moments later with a broad smile upon his face.

A lusty one at that, which made Aislinn's heart skip a beat, her new husband truly more fine-looking than any man had a right to be.

"MacHugh is as welcoming and big-hearted as his niece, good traits for an innkeeper. He'll bed down my horse in the stable, bring us hot water for a bath, aye, and even bring us supper later, if we've a mind for food."

Aislinn felt a rush in her stomach that had nothing to do with any thought of hunger as Cameron lifted her to the ground, his strong hands lingering at her waist.

"Are you happy, wife?"

She bobbed her head, so breathless now that her voice seemed to have fled, while Cameron untied the bag from the saddle, then caught her by the hand and led her into the inn.

CHAPTER 20

Cameron had never felt his heart beat harder as he closed the door behind him and Aislinn—no, not even in the thick of battle!

His gaze swept the modest room with a bed thankfully large enough for two, a wooden tub resting in one corner and the fireplace stacked with logs ready to be lit if the night grew cool, and the shutters already thrown open to the mild breeze by the quick-footed proprietor.

Everything looked clean and well swept, too, which pleased Cameron for he wanted nothing lacking this night—nothing! He had slept on the hard ground or on a simple cot for so much of his life that the room seemed comfortable enough to him, but was Aislinn pleased, too?

He glanced at her, his beautiful bride standing stock-still at his side and staring at the bed.

Her cheeks flushed pink. Her eyes wide. An expression he couldn't read on her face, though he could sense her nervousness as surely as he breathed.

"Aislinn, if you dinna want tae stay here, we can go back tae the MacLeans' and sleep in the barn. I dinna know what the cow and her calf might think—or the goats—"

Her soft laughter had made him fall abruptly silent,

the sound like the sweetest balm to his own nervousness.

Aye, Cameron wanted her so badly that he felt afire from just looking at her, but he was as much an untried virgin as she!

Would he know how to bring her pleasure? Satisfy her? He inwardly cursed the affliction that had kept him from gaining any sexual prowess at all—but he hoped that would please her, too, that he had never lain with any other woman.

Inhaling deeply, Cameron drew her away from the door, wondering if she had gone so far as to think of fleeing. He hoped not—

"It's a fine room, Cameron... so kind of Jeanne and Leith, aye?"

He nodded, relief filling him that she hadn't requested that they return to the farm and a scratchy bed of straw, which made him chuckle now, too.

He had feared the day would never come that he'd feel so at ease with a woman that he could speak with her normally and laugh with her—aye, in spite of his anxiety about what lay ahead. To his surprise, Aislinn reached out and took his hand, her fingers trembling as she looked up at him.

"Forgive me. I... I don't know what to do... how we're to begin..."

His throat tightened at the unshed tears glistening in her eyes, and he took her into his arms, groaning against her hair.

"Forgive *me*, Aislinn. I dinna want tae displease you. I've never bedded a woman... Conall would laugh if he saw me at this moment, aye, and mayhap pity me, too, for thinking that I could disappoint you—"

"Never, Cameron, *never*!" Aislinn lifted her head to stare into his eyes, her hands reaching up to cradle his face. "Everything you've done for me was to please me, to help me, and to help those I love. We'll help each other now, aye? Learn from each other... what pleases me and how I can please you..."

Cameron nearly sank to his knees to hear words from her lips that he'd never thought to hear from any woman... and now Aislinn was his lovely, and so loved, bride. Only a day ago, he had believed her lost to him forever.

He bent his head to kiss her and she met him with parted lips, so soft, so sweet, Cameron sending up a fervent prayer of thanks that she had stowed away and found her way into his life.

He had never felt so blessed, his prayer a plea for protection as well in the days ahead, their path still so uncertain.

He had no idea where they would go next... back to the fortress? Mayhap to MacLachlan Castle where he could seek guidance from Gabriel? Or further north where no one would find them? Och, he didn't want to think of it with Aislinn kissing him with such innocent yearning, her body pressed against him. Later, they must speak of it, but not now. *Not now*!

Cameron groaned against her mouth, his own yearning like a blazing fire that would wait no longer.

Without a word... still kissing her, he released the clasp of her cloak so the garment fell to the floor, and then swept her up and carried her to the bed.

Yet he had no sooner laid her down when he heard a sharp knock, Cameron realizing too late that he hadn't drawn the bolt as Broden cracked open the door.

"Och, Laird, my apologies... but we've hot water for you. Shall we bring it in and fill the tub?"

Cameron nodded, chuckling in spite of himself as Aislinn laughed, too. Her cheeks flushed and her lips a darker rosy hue from his kisses—making him wish so fiercely that he was still kissing her.

He left her with great reluctance and went to throw the door open wide, allowing Broden, a squat balding man, and two serving maids, one as thin as the other was stout, to carry brimming buckets into the room.

The women kept their eyes downcast, though Cameron heard one of them say in a startled aside to the other, "Och, is that a lad or a lass on the bed?"

As both women broke into barely stifled giggles, Cameron strode past them and lifted up the tub with one hand to move it in front of the fireplace—which quieted them down at once, their openly admiring glances now making Aislinn giggle.

"Aye, my husband's a fine, strong man, wouldn't you say?"

Cameron thought the two might drop their buckets at her decidedly feminine voice and exaggerated Irish brogue, though one nudged the other and gave a knowing look as they dumped the steaming water into the tub.

"Och, she's from Éire, that explains it. No bare arses even among the womenfolk."

"See now, no more talk!" sputtered Broden, who emptied his buckets and cast an apologetic look at Cameron while he shooed the women from the room. "We've one more trip tae make—"

"No more trips," Cameron cut him off, striding after them to shut the door. "The tub's full enough." He drew the bolt this time, Broden's raised voice carrying to him from the hall.

"Aye, then, you must let me know if you're wanting anything else."

"We'll do that, MacHugh, our thanks."

Cameron rested his forehead on the door for a moment, laughing under his breath until he heard a splash behind him.

His heart rushed to his throat, he turned around to find Aislinn had thrown off her clothing and jumped into the tub... nothing left but the cloth binding her breasts.

"Would you help me, Cameron?"

In all innocence she sat there, her arms hugging her knees, though from the teasing look in her eyes—och, so blue, *so blue*—he sensed much, if not all, of her nervousness had vanished.

His own had fled, too, Cameron grateful now for the interruption that had proved a godsend for both of them as he walked slowly toward her.

Slowly... because he wanted to feast his eyes on the lithe beauty he'd married, the creamy paleness of her bare skin against the dark wood of the tub making his lower body grow turgid with desire.

Bare skin he wanted to touch, to caress, to kiss... but first, she had made a request of him.

"Och, I see it's knotted," he murmured, his voice thick now at the thought of her full breasts soon to spring free.

Just as slowly, he walked around the tub even as he saw her flesh dimple with goosebumps though steam rose from the water.

Aislinn didn't look up at him, only nodded, and leaned forward so he might reach the knot more easily, Cameron sinking down on one knee behind her and pulling his knife from his belt.

One careful cut and the binding fell away, though he couldn't see her breasts until he drew her backward against the rim—her rosy nipples hard and puckered and glistening with moisture in the sunlight pouring through the window.

With a groan deep in his throat, Cameron knew as well as Aislinn that her bath was suddenly over. She gasped as he stood up and pulled her with him, her body wet and slippery as he carried her to the bed.

Wet and slippery as he laid her down... her eyes widened and her beautiful breasts rising and falling as if she were breathless when he stepped away and threw off his sword belt.

If he had thought her body beyond compare two weeks past when he'd stood by the fireplace as the healer did everything he could to help her—now Cameron could not tear his gaze away from her narrow waist and long limbs and the triangle of soft red curls at the apex of her thighs.

It seemed he had stripped from his clothes before he had drawn another breath, no time for him to bathe, either, as his flesh stood swollen and hard and he knew he could wait no longer to claim her.

Aislinn's gaze had dropped there, too, and she stared at his lower body as if in awe until he climbed atop the bed and blanketed her with his body.

His instincts told him exactly what to do, Cameron parting her legs with his knee and lifting himself up above her.

"It may hurt, love... but only for a moment," he whispered with words that came as if by instinct, too, and then he thrust himself inside her. Aislinn arched her hips against him as she cried out... but only for an instant as she threw her arms around his neck, moaning.

Her eyes wide with wonder, her lips parted, her moans now echoing his as she held onto him tightly, her splayed fingers digging into his back only heightening his pleasure.

His deep thrusts heightening the sound of her pleasure, the two of them moving as one, her breath becoming his breath as Cameron crushed his mouth against hers only to have her kiss him back as fiercely.

Higher and higher they rose together until such a great shuddering swept over them both at the same moment, Aislinn clinging to him and Cameron burying himself deep inside her—that long moments had passed before he found the strength to lift his head.

Aislinn limp beneath him, though her arms were still draped around his neck, languid now as she stared up at him with a look of such sated bliss, Cameron could only stare back in wonder.

She was so... beautiful.

Their bodies still joined, her slender hips moving ever so slightly against his... aye, just enough to make Cameron grow hard and aching for her again... and now it was Aislinn looking up at him in surprise.

"Aye, wife," he murmured, kissing the curve of her cheek, her brow, the tip of her nose. "It seems we both knew exactly what tae do."

Aislinn snuggled deeper into the pillow, smiling to herself at the low rumble of Cameron's breathing at her nape.

He held her so closely that if she moved any more, she might wake him, and she wanted him to sleep. *He needed to sleep!*

Aislinn blushed deeply as she thought of the lovemaking that had carried them well into the night—something awakened in Cameron as if a starving man had been offered a feast.

The first time he had claimed her impassioned and fierce, while the second and third had left her certain there wasn't much of her body that he hadn't kissed and caressed—ah, God.

How could she have known his tongue would bring her such pleasure, such blinding ecstasy?

Aislinn closed her eyes and sighed at the image in her mind of Cameron lowering his head between her splayed thighs and burying his face into the very heart of her... making her tremble now at the remembering.

She bit her lower lip and told herself again to lie still and think of anything else so that she wouldn't rouse him. Yet how could she not think of the intimacy of his touch when he had his arm securely around her waist, his head resting on her shoulder, and his lower body pressed against her bottom?

At once another heart-stopping vision came to her... Cameron standing naked beside the bed and looking more magnificent than she could have ever imagined.

His swollen flesh erect against a thatch of black hair and an abdomen so powerfully muscled that she had stared at him in wonder—yet not for long.

A breathless moment more and he had joined her on the bed and covered her wet body with his own. Any chill she had felt vanishing at the heated sensation of his flesh against hers... no, no, she must stop!

Aislinn had to stifle another sigh at the lustiness of her thoughts and told herself she must get some more sleep, too, but even now, the warmth of Cameron's body burned into hers.

She tried to distract herself by glancing around the dimly lit room, the logs burned down to glowing embers, but everywhere she looked aroused vivid images to make her shiver...

Cameron getting up from the bed to close the shutters at the windows, affording her a view of his broad back and taut buttocks.

Cameron lighting the logs in the fireplace to ward off the early evening chill, and opening the door only enough to shout down the stairs that a hot supper would be welcome.

While they had waited, he had astonished her by standing in the tub—not big enough for her strapping husband to sit—and bathing in water that had long since grown cold.

He had laughed and told her that it wasn't as frigid as lochs and creeks where he'd washed himself over the years, and then he had beckoned to her to join him, but Aislinn had shook her head and ducked under the covers.

Laughing, too, but she had shrieked when he pulled

her out of the bed and carried her to the tub where he bade her huskily to stand as well.

Aislinn had been amazed that she'd hardly felt the water's chill for Cameron's hands rubbing a sliver of wild thyme-scented soap over her body.

Her breasts, her belly... and between her legs where he had lingered... teasing a quivering response from her that left her moaning and certain that her knees would buckle until he drew her into his arms to kiss her at the height of her release.

Aye, how was she to fall asleep again with such rousing memories tumbling through her mind?

Aislinn inhaled deeply and stretched in contentment against Cameron in spite of her resolve to lie still.

The only thing that had passed by in a blur was supper. She remembered Cameron accepting a tray through the door, the stout serving maid wide-eyed at his nakedness, which had made them both laugh. Yet food had seemed so inconsequential to the burning kisses and caresses that came after, until a satiated exhaustion had overcome them—

"What are you thinking of, wife?"

Aislinn gasped as Cameron eased her onto her back and began to nuzzle her ear, her throat, while she could only answer truthfully, "You, husband."

She reached up to stroke the dark stubble along his cheek, which made him clasp her hand and press a kiss into her palm. She drew in her breath, such a rush of emotion filling her heart, which seemed to be echoed by the way he stared down at her.

"I love you, Aislinn Campbell."

He didn't give her a chance to answer, Cameron lowering his head and kissing her until she felt breathless, his tongue teasing her lips apart and sweeping into her mouth.

She felt his desire flaring hot again, and she curled

her arms around his neck to pull him closer, which made him groan against her mouth.

A sudden thought drifting to her, aye, a wish, a prayer that their lovemaking on this night, their first as husband and wife, might bless them with a child —ah, God!

Aislinn stiffened, another unbidden thought following, which made Cameron stop kissing her and lift his head.

"Aislinn?"

She couldn't answer, tears burning her eyes as Aengus Butler's words flew back to haunt her.

I want strong sons—not weaklings like your pitiful brother—and seed growing inside your belly will accomplish my aim whether it's that Highlander's or mine.

Heaven help her, a premonition? She held no hope at all that he had sailed back to Ireland without her. Was Aengus looking for her now... mayhap somewhere near?

"Aislinn, what's wrong? Tell me!"

She opened her mouth to speak, but a sudden pounding at the door made her freeze in Cameron's arms.

CHAPTER 21

"Laird, you and your lady must wake!"

Cameron was already lunging from the bed to grab his sword, the fear in Broden MacHugh's voice making the hairs prickle at the back of his neck.

"English marauders, Laird! Word has come that they've raided farms all around this night—stealing food and livestock, aye, and mayhap women as well."

"Ah, no, Cameron, the MacLeans!"

Aislinn's voice stricken, he reached out to help her from the bed as he shouted to Broden, "We're up, man! Bring round my horse."

Cameron could see tears glistening in Aislinn's eyes in the low firelight, but those had been there before Broden had brought them such wretched news. Yet there was no time to press her further about what had distressed her.

Those marauders might be bearing down soon upon the village—och, he could only hope that they had gained enough spoils from their treacherous night's work to have returned to wherever they had come from. Mayhap the garrison where those English soldiers that had taken Sorcha had been quartered?

Cursing the Scots nobles who still supported King Edward by allowing his forces to occupy their land and castles, Cameron laid his sword upon the bed and drew Aislinn into his arms.

"We'll have tae stay off the road and skirt along the woods so we can seek cover."

"I understand," she murmured, her voice shaking with distress. "The ride will take us longer."

"Aye. It's near dawn, so we'll pray that the marauders are done with their raid and heading home—though I wish tae God I had men enough with me tae find them and cut them all down."

"Ah, God... Sorcha, Jeanne..."

"No, we canna think the worst." Cameron pulled Aislinn closer and felt her shivering as if from cold. "Aislinn, I know something distressed you, but we must dress and go quickly—"

"I was praying this night might bring us a babe... and then I thought of Aengus and that he doesn't care if a child would be yours or his. A fear came to me that he might be near, looking for me—but it's the English."

"Aye, and if they've not gone home, then mayhap the village is next. You must get dressed, Aislinn—*now*!"

Cameron had spoken sternly, but every moment they lingered was another drawing them closer to danger. There was only one of him—aye, he could fight off a dozen men, but if there were more?

To his relief, Aislinn went to gather up her clothing and dress, and he did the same. Another few moments and he pulled open the door, his sword drawn, while she held a knife in her hand.

A second one he'd given her, her face pale in the lamplight as they hastened down the stairs and outside into a scene of pure bedlam.

Frightened women and children with what possessions they could carry were fleeing for the nearby woods, some pulling along bleating sheep and goats, while the men had gathered in the center of the village.

Some holding swords and spears while others had

grabbed pitchforks and whatever else they could use as weapons, Cameron never feeling more torn as he mounted his snorting horse and pulled Aislinn up behind him.

"Godspeed, Laird!" cried Broden above the clamor, his face pale, too, in the light from the brightening sky. "Another rider just brought word that the marauders themselves were attacked by a large force of men riding south. Most of the English were killed, but we're ready tae fight if any remnants dare come near."

"Good man, fight for Scotland!" Cameron veered his horse around, saying over his shoulder to Aislinn, "Hold on tight."

She did, gripping him around the waist as they rode from the village, Cameron not wanting her in front of him this time for the hard pace they must set.

He had come so close to telling her that they must stay and fight alongside the innkeeper and the others, but Broden's startling news had changed everything.

A large force riding to the south? If they had thrashed the English marauders, then they had to be supporters of King Robert. And that meant any women seized would have been rescued, unless they had been defiled and left for dead outside their homes—

"Ride, Cameron, *ride*!"

Aislinn's voice ragged, desperate, she must have guessed his grim thoughts.

He urged his steed into a hard gallop, no need any longer to skirt the woods as clods of dirt kicked up from the road rained down behind them.

~

"No... oh, God, no!" Aislinn had smelled the acrid stench of smoke long before she and Cameron came upon the devastation, the MacLeans' sod-roofed house and barn reduced to smoldering rubble.

A few trampled chickens lay scattered in the dirt, poor Speckles among them, while the others were gone from the coop, the marauders having taken them.

Aislinn didn't wait for Cameron to bring his steed to a stop before she slipped from the saddle and stood there in the yard, gazing in horror around her.

She judged from the devastation that Leith and Jeanne's farm must have been one of the first attacked deep in the night... the fire set hours ago by the English. Yet what had become of the family—no, she couldn't bear to think of it.

"Aislinn... over there by the barn."

Cameron had dismounted, too, his sword in hand as he strode toward a motionless body upon the ground while Aislinn ran to catch up with him.

He reached out as if to catch her and prevent her from drawing closer, but she rushed past him and stopped short at the terrible sight of Leith's mangled remains.

His throat cut. His body trampled into the ground like the chickens, Aislinn feeling certain that she was going to vomit.

"Ah, God, Cameron... no." Choking down bile, she met his eyes, but he didn't look at all as if he were about to be sick.

His face darkened, his sword clenched in his fist, he looked... enraged.

"If any of those bastards still live and have been taken prisoner, I swear I will find them and kill them myself."

Aislinn didn't doubt it, his voice as harsh as she'd ever heard it while she glanced around them in despair.

She saw no other bodies, yet, and told herself that she must take a closer look around the fire-blackened ruins—as Cameron appeared to be doing—but she felt rooted to the ground.

Here they had saved Sorcha from a heinous fate,

only to suffer this one? Was there no mercy in heaven for so sweet a young girl and her kind-hearted mother? Her father slain, Jeanne's beloved husband—dear God, Aislinn prayed not right in front of them.

Somehow she forced herself to move and follow after Cameron, who walked around the perimeter of the destruction... clearly looking for what Aislinn prayed even more fiercely they would not find.

With those marauders slain, then the women would have been rescued, aye? If Sorcha and Jeanne had been taken as captives, please may it be so. *Please—*

"Aislinn, did you hear that?"

Cameron had stopped cold to glance into the trees, the closest ones scorched, too, from the fire. His hand raised as if asking her for silence. She didn't move, either, but stared as well in the same direction and listened...

"Aye, there it is again—weeping!"

Her heart hammering in her throat, Aislinn rushed after him as he plunged into the trees, his sword brandished in front of him while she pulled out the knife he had given her.

Yet she no sooner had the weapon gripped in her hand when she sheathed it again... slowing her pace in shock at the sight of Sorcha leaning against a tree and crying as if her heart would break.

Cameron reached her before Aislinn and swept the girl into his arms, his voice so low and consoling that tears welled in her eyes.

Her beloved husband... so forbidding and fearsome a warrior with moisture in his eyes, too, as Sorcha clung to him.

"It's all right, child, we're here. You're safe now," he sought to soothe her as Aislinn rushed to embrace her as well, the three of them standing there together.

Yet Sorcha would not be consoled, her tear-stained face flushed from crying as she twisted herself free from both of them and pointed deeper into the woods.

"Mama, she's out there! Papa saw the English coming and told us tae run and hide and we did, as fast as we could. But she tripped over a log and there was a terrible crack—ah, please, you must help her! We heard your voices through the trees and Mama told me tae find you—"

"Lead the way, Sorcha, that's a brave lass," Cameron cut in gently, glancing at Aislinn. "Hold her hand and walk with her, love, and I'll follow you."

Aislinn nodded and obliged him at once, such relief flooding her to know that Jeanne, too, was alive. Sorcha fairly pulled her along, the child was so desperate to reach her mother, Aislinn taking care not to trip herself over scattered branches and rocks.

Yet she felt the blood rush from her face as soon as she heard Jeanne's pain-wracked moaning, Sorcha once again bursting into tears.

Cameron lunged past them and reached the prone woman first, and dropped to his knees beside her.

"God help us," was all he said, Aislinn feeling her stomach pitch again at the sight of shattered white bone sticking out of Jeanne's lower right leg.

As Sorcha ran to her mother's side and threw her arms around Jeanne's neck, Aislinn could see, too, that she'd had the presence of mind to rip away the hem of her tunic to try and staunch the bleeding... though the mossy ground was dark with dried blood.

Cameron at once tore off his breacan. With low comforting words to Jeanne, he tore the garment in two and wrapped one piece securely around her lower leg.

"It will hurt, Jeanne, but I must tighten the cloth into a knot."

As the woman nodded and focused upon her daughter's face, Aislinn could see the terrible pain she suffered as Cameron worked to secure the cloth over the break and then knot the other piece above her knee, but Jeanne didn't utter a sound. Aislinn unclasped her cloak and handed it to Cameron, who settled the garment around Jeanne's shoulders.

Did she know what had happened to her husband? Sorcha, to her father? Aislinn doubted it since he had told them to run, which clearly had saved them from the marauders. Yet for this terrible injury to happen as well?

"That's all we can do for now." Sighing heavily, Cameron glanced at Aislinn and then back to Jeanne. "Is there a healer in the village? I can take you there—"

"No, Laird, he died a month past. An old man, so there's no one now."

"Then we've a longer ride ahead of us, but I will find you help, I promise you. Aislinn, you and Sorcha will take the pony—"

"Pony?" Staring at Cameron, she followed his gaze deep into the trees to the right and saw the sturdy pony she had ridden from the convent nibbling on some grass.

"Aye, he had enough wits about him tae run, too. Jeanne, are you willing tae ride fast? The pain will be great, but if we do, we'll be in Dumbarton in a few hours' time—"

"*Dumbarton*, Cameron?" Stunned, Aislinn felt as if she stared stupidly at him again, but his grim nod told her that he knew well the risks.

"We've no choice, wife... not if she's tae have a chance tae live. If anyone can tend tae her, it's King Robert's healers. They've seen far worse from battle, believe me."

He didn't wait for a reply, but rose and lifted Jeanne with him, her outcry of pain scattering a flock of blackbirds high up in the trees.

"Och, forgive me, Laird—"

MIRIAM MINGER

"You've nothing tae forgive. You must know, Jeanne, your husband—"

"Aye, he's with God... and I know, too, Laird, we've no time for a burial. My daughter's without her father now, and I'll pray she willna lose me, too—"

"Dinna think the worst," Cameron said with another glance at Aislinn, his words echoing the ones he'd said to her at the inn. "The pony, love..."

Warmed by his endearment, she could tell nonetheless by the lines etching his handsome face in the morning sunlight filtering through the leaves that he hadn't stopped thinking about what might lie ahead for them. Yet what else could be done? They couldn't just leave Jeanne at the village to die.

As Sorcha followed after Cameron and her mother, Aislinn hastened to fetch the pony, which turned his head and nickered at her as she approached him.

"Aye, I'm taking you back to where you came from," she murmured, grasping his thick mane as she had done before and hoisting herself onto his back. "Good boy, get on with you. You've run fast as the wind for me before, so let's see you do it again."

CHAPTER 22

"I fear Jeanne doesna have long, Aislinn. She's asking for you... aye, Laird Campbell as well."

Aislinn nodded at Sister Agnes, who kept her arm around Sorcha's waist and guided the sobbing girl out the door of the nuns' quarters for some fresh air.

Aislinn glanced at Cameron, his face bearing the sorrow they both felt—and she knew he blamed himself, too.

Jeanne's pain had grown too great for them to make it all the way to Dumbarton Castle, so they had ridden to the convent instead. Sister Agnes had taken them in at once, Jeanne made comfortable in the same room where Aislinn had convalesced... except now there would be no convalescing for Sorcha's mother.

She had lost too much blood before they had found her in the woods, Aislinn blinking back tears at how brave Jeanne had been while they had ridden south as fast as they could.

Never once crying out in pain.

Her eyes, when opened, focused upon Sorcha holding onto Aislinn as they rode beside Cameron's larger steed, the stout-hearted pony able to keep up because Cameron had held his horse back so they wouldn't fall behind.

"We should have taken her tae the village," Cameron murmured, his voice heavy with regret as they stood together outside Jeanne's room. "I dinna know why I thought there was hope. I knew her injury would threaten her life the moment I saw it."

"You wanted tae find her help, husband, a noble plan—a kind and caring plan," Aislinn countered, taking his hand. "Come, love, she's asking for us."

Cameron's grim expression easing at the endearment, which until now he'd been the only one to use, he squeezed her hand and walked with her into the room.

At once Sister Hestia rose from a chair near the bed, the nun's plain, pinched features marked by sadness. "She's very weak... here, I'll move the chair closer for you, Aislinn."

The scraping of the chair legs upon the wooden floor seemed to rouse Jeanne, who turned her head from the mullioned window as Aislinn sat down beside her.

Cameron drew closer, too, while Sister Hestia left them in a soft flutter of black habit and closed the door behind her as Jeanne began to speak with great effort.

"Laird Campbell... Aislinn... I've a grievous sin weighing upon my soul. You must hear me while there's still time."

Aislinn nodded and took Jeanne's outstretched hand, the dying woman's fingers so cold that she had to blink away tears.

"Ah, sweet lass, dinna cry for me. I'll be with my Leith again soon, aye, and he's already answered for our sin... but what else could we have done?"

Jeanne glanced with despair from Aislinn to Cameron, who went down on one knee beside the bed to cover their hands with his own, his fingers so warm and comforting.

"You're a good, kind woman," he said gently, as if to reassure her. "No sin of yours could be so grave—"

"Ah, but we kept Sorcha for our own daughter when we should have tried tae find her kin. Yet there was no one tae ask—all those poor drowned souls upon the beach. Leith and I couldna believe when we heard a wee bairn crying... but there she was, tangled in sea-weed. An older woman lying dead next tae her, the child's nurse, surely—och, God!"

Jeanne had tried to sit up in the telling, but had fallen back onto the pillow, gasping with pain as Aislinn leaned closer.

"So you kept the child when the rest were dead, surely that's no sin—"

"Aye, it was! We heard others coming tae gather what they could from the shipwreck and we ran away with her. I couldna have bairns of my own, you see? We lived further south near Leith's kinsmen, but we kept her hidden and moved north tae start a new life—"

"Ease yourself, Jeanne, her parents must have drowned, too," Cameron interrupted her gently. "You and Leith did the best you could by her. If you hadna found her when you did, the waves would have dragged her back into the sea."

As if his words had lifted a great weight from her shoulders, Jeanne heaved a weak sigh, the last of her strength spent. Aislinn felt her fingers growing limp, though the woman fixed her dimming gaze upon them.

"Please... take Sorcha with you and raise her as your own. Swear tae me, I beg you..."

"Aye, I swear it."

Cameron answering first, his voice low and resolute, Aislinn met his eyes as she nodded. "Aye, I swear it."

She could not say if Jeanne even heard her for the rasping sounds coming from the woman's chest... though a faint smile had settled upon Jeanne's lips as she drew a shallow breath, and then another... and then fell still.

Neither Aislinn nor Cameron spoke for a long moment, Aislinn laying Jeanne's lifeless hand upon the bed. A soft rap at the door made him rise to his feet and draw Aislinn up beside him to pull her into his arms.

"Sorcha canna know the truth, Aislinn. It would crush her. Someday mayhap we'll tell her, but Leith and Jeanne MacLean will always be her loved parents, aye?"

"Aye, Cameron."

He bent his head to kiss her with such tenderness as the door opened, Sister Agnes having returned with Sorcha while Sister Hestia stood behind them.

All the girl had to do was look into Aislinn's eyes and she burst into anguished sobs, Sorcha running into the room to sink to her knees beside the bed... her small hand reaching out to touch Jeanne's face.

"Mama... *Mama*!"

"Let's give the lass a few moments with her mother," Cameron said as he drew Aislinn into the hallway, though she wanted so badly to stay and comfort her.

He looked so grim again that she felt a chill. Sister Agnes followed them after murmuring to Sister Hestia to remain with Sorcha, and then she shut the door quietly against her heartbreaking cries.

"Please... a word."

Aislinn felt Cameron's hand clench around hers, which made her think that he must sense what Sister Agnes might have to say to them.

"What will you do now, Laird? You have a wife tae think of... and a family now."

"You heard us?"

Startled by the harshness in Cameron's voice, Aislinn was relieved when Sister Agnes shook her head that she hadn't been listening through the door.

"Jeanne shared with me—and Sorcha—that she hoped you would take her with you and raise her as your daughter. Yet you have a terrible man that wishes tae destroy you, Laird. If you could have heard Lord Butler when he learned that Aislinn had run away from the convent—God help me! I've never wished ill on any soul, but I prayed hard from then on that he never came face-tae-face with either of you ever again. What will happen now? Where will you go?"

Cameron didn't readily answer, his jaw clenched, his grip almost painful upon Aislinn's hand, until he sighed with great heaviness.

"Forgive me, Reverend Mother. It's Aengus Butler who plagues my mind, not you. Aye, we both swore tae Jeanne that we'd take Sorcha, but I canna say what will happen when Aislinn and I return tae Dumbarton Castle."

"*Dumbarton Castle?*" Aislinn echoed, stunned. "We don't have to go there now. I would have done anything to help Jeanne, God rest her, but she would want us to think of Sorcha—"

"I *am* thinking of Sorcha—and you, wife." Cameron met her eyes, his voice low and fierce. "I canna trust that our riding tae even the northernmost reaches of Scotland will stop Lord Butler from coming after you—and I believe only King Robert has been standing in his way. He gave me three days tae bring you back, Aislinn, and I will honor his command and not defy him. Will you go with me now and not fight me?"

Aislinn swallowed hard and nodded, though she felt a deeper chill grip her. "Aye, Cameron, I'll not fight you... but if I should lose you—"

"Or I you," Cameron cut her off, his darkened eyes blazing into hers, "but we willna think of it, agreed? We must trust that God doesna want us parted—Reverend Mother, will you pray for us?"

"Every moment," Sister Agnes blurted, crossing herself and then pressing her lips to the gold crucifix she wore around her neck. "I'll keep Sorcha here with us, aye? Until you come back for her... both of you."

Cameron nodded grimly and led the way, Aislinn

hastening with him as the piteous sound of Sorcha's weeping followed them out the door.

~

Cameron had fully intended to ride hard to Dumbarton, the town and fortress a good five leagues away. Yet once outside the convent gate, he clasped Aislinn tightly against him and breathed in the sun-warmed scent of her hair.

She sat in the saddle in front of him, which is where he wanted her so that he could hold her close and whisper into her ear how much he loved her—aye, just as he did now.

In answer, she leaned her head back against his shoulder and said quietly, "I love you, Laird Campbell," her mood as subdued as Cameron's even though they had Sister Agnes's fervent prayers surrounding them.

He didn't want to think about what might come in spite of a burning hope that King Robert would not wrest Aislinn from him.

Lord Butler might support the fight for independence from England, but the king knew the character of the Irishman from his coarse words and actions. Surely that Aislinn was his wife's cousin would grant her royal protection—aye, Cameron had to believe that it would be so.

"That's the wall I climbed over when I ran from the convent."

Cameron glanced to where Aislinn pointed, his stallion pricking up his ears and snorting, which made her laugh softly.

"Aye, jumping to the ground knocked the wind from me… and there's the farm where I borrowed the pony. I'm glad Sister Agnes already had one of the nuns return him. Ah, look, he's grazing with his companions."

Indeed, the sturdy pony appeared to be contentedly

back at home and munching grass, and looking none the worse for his adventure.

Not so for poor Jeanne, Cameron couldn't help thinking, and Aislinn's plaintive sigh told him she was thinking of Sorcha's mother, too.

A well-tended cemetery lay outside the convent walls, where Jeanne would be laid to rest before nightfall. Already well into the afternoon, the sunlight that had felt so warm when he and Aislinn had mounted his steed moments ago, had disappeared behind dark clouds scudding across the sky.

Aye, why not a storm to add more misery to the day? Cameron had never *not* known the weather to change quickly, many a battle fought in mud up to his knees when a morning had dawned bright and clear.

He no longer had his breacan, which he'd used to wrap Jeanne's leg, and Aislinn had left her cloak spread upon the woman's bed to give her more warmth—och, so nothing to throw over their heads.

A sudden crack of thunder right above them made Cameron curse as his stallion reared up, squealing, while Aislinn was jolted hard against his chest.

Somehow they both kept their seats, but another deafening boom and a blinding flash of lightning made him clench the reins and hold her even more tightly as he veered his horse toward a rocky outcropping in the distance.

They were nearly there when the blackened sky opened up into a lashing downpour, both of them drenched by the time they reached cover.

Aislinn, though, didn't seem dismayed at all as they dismounted and Cameron tethered his horse under one side of the outcropping, but laughed as if with exhilaration.

He had only to draw closer to see that he'd misjudged her emotion, for tears streamed down her face, melding with the wetness from the rain.

"Aislinn..." He pulled her into his arms and let her weep, her shoulders quaking.

Aye, why wouldn't she need to cry after Jeanne's death and with the weight of uncertainty that faced them?

His beloved Aislinn, so bold and courageous and yet with a tender heart, too.

Such emotion overcame him as well to hear her anguish that he pressed a kiss against her damp cheek and held her even closer. A few moments more and her sobs quieted, her arms going round him to hug him as tightly.

The thunder now a distant rumbling and lightning no longer flashing, the downpour lessened to a steady soft rain that seemed to lull him even as Aislinn lifted her head to look into his eyes.

"If I lose you, Cameron, I don't want to live."

Och, God, he could have uttered the same thing— but instead he stroked her cheek, his throat so tight that it felt painful for him to speak.

"Dinna say such a thing, wife, for what if we've made a sweet bairn together? A sister or brother for Sorcha—"

"How will she ever know if I'm forced to return to Éire? Never to see you again! Never to hold you again or kiss you—"

Cameron's mouth upon hers silenced her, Aislinn kissing him back with such aching despair that he groaned against her lips—vowing to himself that he would die before ever allowing such a thing to happen. *Aye, he would protect her to his last breath*!

Shaking with emotion, Cameron lifted her bodily and pressed her against the rock wall... one hand supporting her while the other slid beneath her tunic to yank her trousers to below her hips.

Aislinn grasping wildly at his tunic to pull the front

of his garment up as well, Cameron driving himself into her as she moaned against his mouth.

Her arms flying around him to clasp his shoulders. Her fingers digging into his back while he thrust deeply inside her, Cameron never lifting his mouth from hers.

Her anguish now his anguish... though deep in his heart as he spilled himself into her, Aislinn crying out his name with her own shuddering release... Cameron felt a glimmer of hope that God would somehow protect them, too.

CHAPTER 23

"**C** ameron!"

Aislinn heard Conall's voice before she saw him—but from Cameron's low curse, he must have seen his brother right away as Conall ran toward them across the bailey.

A windswept bailey noisy with commotion that grew eerily silent but for the whinnying of horses when she and Cameron rode through the gates of Dumbarton Castle.

The muddy expanse leading to the fortress built at the base of a towering rock was packed with men and horses, too, and Cameron had seemed certain that King Robert's forces were on alert for an imminent attack from King Edward.

That is, until he recognized some of the faces surrounding them, Cameron sounding startled as he reined in his horse and murmured to her, "Those are Gabriel's men—och, and that group over there, Rory Campbell's men."

"Rory Campbell?"

"Aye, the chieftain of Clan Campbell, my cousin."

Cameron didn't have a chance to say more as Conall reached them, a strange mix of gladness and apprehension on his face as he glanced from Aislinn to his elder brother.

"Och, man, you couldna have arrived at a more contentious moment. I had tae step outside for some air, the rancor got so thick—and here you are! The both of you."

Aislinn could feel tension growing in Cameron as he scowled at Conall and dismounted, and then reached up to lift her to the ground.

"The king gave me three days tae bring her back tae Dumbarton, did he not? You heard what the messenger said when last I saw you."

"Aye, brother, but you said your plan was tae head north when you found Aislinn—"

"What does it matter? We're here now—but why are *you* here, Conall? By God, did you leave anyone in command of the fortress?"

Aislinn saw Conall stiffen as if affronted, though he kept his voice steady.

"Aye, Finlay's there, and Alun's in command at Mac-Lachlan Castle. We came here tae plead for you, Cameron. Myself, Gabriel, and Magdalene—and they're in the great hall at this very moment, making an appeal tae King Robert that he allow you and Aislinn tae wed."

Aislinn gaped at Conall, a giggle escaping her before she could clap her hand over her mouth, though she knew the situation wasn't humorous at all.

At once she felt Cameron's hand at her waist and he gave a short laugh, too, while Conall looked from her flushed face to Cameron... his eyes widening with understanding.

"Are you wed, then?" Now Conall laughed as Aislinn smiled at Cameron, her face burning even hotter. "Och, what am I asking? Look at the two of you... as sick in love as any I've seen. Forgive me, brother. I should have given my support instead of railing at you like a fool, but I feared for you—aye, still do. Lord Butler is inside—"

"No, I don't want to see him!" Aislinn blurted out, reaching for Cameron's hand to entwine her fingers tightly with his. All humor had fled, replaced only by dread as she met his darkened gaze. "What are we to do?"

"Face him. Let's have this thing done."

Cameron sounded so grim that she shivered, as much that her clothes were still wet from the rain that had thankfully stopped, as that she feared for him, too.

"Conall, will you spare her your breacan? We got caught in the storm."

"Aye, brother."

Conall unwound the garment from his waist and left shoulder, his expression grown as somber as Cameron's. "A fierce storm, indeed, but no more earsplitting than Butler's howls of protest when Gabriel told the king what we were about. Rory Campbell isna pleased, either, Cameron. He's here tae demand that you wed one of our clanswomen—aye, it seems Uncle Torence wasna too drunk after all."

Aislinn glanced up gratefully as Cameron wrapped the breacan around her shoulders, only to see his jaw clenched at this news.

"He overheard us?"

"Aye. He knew you'd rode off and he sent one of his men right after tae Rory. Our chief might have found you, too, if not for the English they came upon and routed. Seems the bastards had been riding through the countryside, stealing women and livestock."

"So my kinsmen slew the marauders... though not soon enough tae spare the MacLeans, God rest them."

Aislinn swallowed hard at the dark glance between Cameron and Conall, who clearly grasped the import of his brother's words and looked sickened.

"The whole family?"

"Their young daughter still lives," Aislinn interjected sadly as Cameron guided her toward the entrance to the keep, Conall striding alongside them. "We left her at the convent until we return—ah, God, Cameron, wait!"

Heated voices had carried to her, a harsh and furious one rising above the rest, which made her fling her arms around Cameron and hug him tightly.

He hugged her back with the fiercest embrace, though he said nothing, only kissed her brow and then brushed his lips against hers all too briefly.

He looked fearsome, resolute, his mind already fixed upon what lay ahead. Aislinn felt her heart rush to her throat when he released her to grip the hilt of his sword with one hand and her trembling fingers with the other —aye, she was shaking.

"Come."

She did, Conall gripping his sword, too. He moved ahead of them as if by some unspoken agreement with Cameron... and turned first into the great hall.

"My lord king! My brother Laird Cameron Campbell and his wedded wife, Aislinn Campbell!"

Conall's ringing announcement both bold and triumphant, Aislinn drew in her breath as the clamor of voices came to an immediate—and stunned—halt.

Everyone looking at them... aye, King Robert, who stood on a dais next to his throne with guards not far from him.

The strapping dark-haired warrior Aislinn judged to be Gabriel MacLachlan, whose hand went at once to his sword as he drew his beautiful wife against him.

Magdalene's eyes wide with astonishment... and then she lifted her chin and smiled at Aislinn as if ecstatic.

Another warrior neither as tall nor as broad-shouldered as Cameron and Conall, though he bore the same midnight hair and formidable demeanor—aye, Rory, the chieftain of Clan Campbell, who didn't look pleased at all.

Somehow Aislinn lifted her chin, too, as Aengus Butler's enraged curse seemed to shake the rafters... while her brother, Daran, standing next to the man, flinched and seemed to cower.

"Come closer!"

King Robert's raised voice as ringing as Conall's, Aislinn doubted she would have moved if not for Cameron's hand drawing her forward.

"Consummated?" the king queried bluntly, stepping down from the dais to stride toward them.

"Aye, my lord king." Cameron's reply as blunt, he nonetheless squeezed Aislinn's fingers as if to reassure her. "We married in a village church two hours' ride north with a priest presiding and another cleric as witness—our names written in the parish register. We spent our wedding night at an inn there—"

"I care not if you plowed her in the road," Aengus Butler spat out, his hand clenching the hilt of his sword. "I demand an annulment at once!"

"You *demand*?" King Robert rounded on him, and gestured for several stoic-faced guards to flank the Irishman, Daran shrinking back behind him. "You forget yourself, Lord Butler. This is my dominion—and I say that congratulations, *not* censure, are in order."

"*Congratulations?*" Aengus countered, clearly not intimidated at all by the king. "You contrived for this to happen... refusing first to grant your consent for my men and me to ride north in search of the wench—"

"My *wife*," Cameron cut in harshly, while Aislinn winced now at how tightly he gripped her hand as if Aengus might attempt to wrench her from him. "Enough, Butler! The marriage is done and not tae be undone by you. It's time for you tae board your ship and return tae Éire and plague us no more. *What therefore God hath joined together, let not man put asunder—*"

"Bastard! You dare to quote Holy Scripture to me when you've stolen my bride?" Aengus's face florid with fury, spittle foaming at the corners of his mouth, he drew his sword only to have two guards grab his arms, the weapon clattering to the floor.

Yet it was his scream of rage that made a chill plummet through Aislinn, the man wresting himself free like a maddened bull and rushing not at Cameron, but at her.

She was knocked to the ground, Aengus sprawling on top of her and grabbing for her throat—only to have Cameron hurl the man aside so violently that he lost his own balance and fell right in front of her.

The breath knocked from him in a terrible whoosh even as Aengus pulled a knife from his belt and lunged at Cameron's chest.

She didn't think, only reacted, scrambling onto her knees to unsheathe Cameron's sword and wield it above her to deflect the oncoming blow. Metal struck metal as shouts rent the air, the guards, Conall, and Gabriel rushing forward with their weapons raised.

Another one reaching Aengus first, Daran's anguished voice calling out her name as Aislinn saw the flash of a sword out of the corner of her eye.

Aengus's scream not of rage but of high-pitched disbelief, the man crumpling to the floor in a gush of blood.

His head half severed from his body, his arms and legs twitching in death as Cameron hauled Aislinn against him to hold her close... kissing her tear-streaked face, her hair.

"My warrior wife... my protector..."

Only then did she drop the sword beside them, Aislinn having clenched the weapon so tightly that her cramped fingers would not uncurl. Cameron brought her hand to his mouth and kissed her reddened palm, too, while King Robert's voice boomed around them.

"By God, De Burgh, you'll make one of my finest fighters yet!"

Aislinn glanced up at Daran, her brother standing taller and straighter than she had ever seen him as Gabriel and Conall clapped him on the back... even Rory coming up to praise him.

"So, Campbell, will you accept this marriage and wish them happiness?" King Robert said in a command more than a query, coming forward himself to help Cameron to his feet, Aislinn rising beside him. "She's my beloved wife's cousin, after all. What finer honor for your clan than this union between my family and yours, aye?"

"Aye, my lord king."

Rory Campbell's answer not grudging at all, the chieftain even smiled wryly at Cameron.

"You'd do well not tae argue with the lass, cousin— or you'll find yourself at the tip of a sword."

Aislinn might have smiled, too, if not for King Robert's guards dragging away Aengus's body while servants rushed to wipe up the blood... though the men around her seemed not to spare the dead man a glance.

"It's commonplace tae them... death," came a soft voice beside her. Magdalene reached out to clasp Aislinn's hand, her sea green eyes shining. "They're warriors, our husbands... but we're fighters, too, in our own way. I think you and I are going tae be great friends, aye?"

Aislinn nodded as Gabriel came over to claim his wife and Cameron drew her close against him, though at that moment, her eyes were fixed upon someone else... Daran.

Cameron seemed to read her mind. He brushed a kiss to her cheek and released her so that Aislinn could go to her brother, tears of gratitude brimming in her eyes.

Daran no longer appearing a cowering youth, but a

man... both of them freed from the painful past with their father, though Aislinn inwardly wished him peace.

"If not for you, I might have lost all," she began, but her throat tightened so much that it took her a moment to continue. "My life... my love—"

"You're as brave as they come," Daran interrupted her quietly, drawing her into his arms to embrace her. "I'm proud that you're my sister, Aislinn. Forgive me for not speaking up on your behalf before Papa died, aye, even after... and for allowing you to suffer. I've known all along that you were the stronger one."

"Saints help us, no longer, Daran." Wiping the tears from her eyes, she stepped back to gaze at him proudly. "What will you do now? Return to Éire?"

He shook his head and glanced over at King Robert, who stood surrounded by Campbells. "I came here to fight. Father's estate is well tended and doesn't need me there—"

"*Your* estate. You're Lord De Burgh now. One day you'll go back, but for now—if you wish to accompany us to Campbell Castle, you could train with some of the most renowned warriors in Scotland."

"Aye, and we'll practice how not tae lose one's footing," Cameron said wryly, coming up behind Aislinn. "Och, mayhap I'm getting old..."

"Not old at all," she countered, thrilling at the weight of his hands around her waist to pull her against him. "Just not invincible, much as any other man... but magnificent all the same. *I* should know."

Throwing back his head, Cameron laughed, a full rich sound melding with her own that she hoped and prayed they would share more of together. Yet she quieted as another thought struck her that made him grow sober, too, as if he knew exactly what was on her mind.

"Aye, let's get back tae Sorcha. Our daughter needs us today."

"Your daughter?" Daran echoed, Aislinn nodding and reaching out to take his hand.

"Ride with us and I'll tell you all along the way—"

"So are my warriors soon tae return tae their posts?" King Robert's raised voice interrupted her. "I need you in Argyll tae prevent the MacDougalls from trying tae regain power... not here making appeals and taking brides!"

He roared with laughter now, all the clamor and strife clearly having exhilarated him.

It made perfect sense to Aislinn that this powerful, indomitable man was King of Scotland as a chorus of full-throated "Ayes!" answered his query, which made tears rush to her eyes. She left Cameron and her brother and ran to give King Robert a hug, startling him, though he didn't appear displeased.

"Thank you, my lord king!"

"Och, lass, go back tae your fine husband with my blessing. I knew the moment I heard you'd fled the convent that the two of you were destined tae wed—aye, with a wee bit of my help. There's no sense standing in the way of a red-haired Irishwoman!"

CHAPTER 24

"**D**o you think he'll like it?"

At Aislinn's soft query, Sorcha nodded and clapped her hands together, her eyes alight as Aislinn slowly turned in a circle.

The silk of her emerald green gown swishing softly while her matching slippers made no sound upon the thick rug.

Since she and Cameron had arrived back at Campbell Castle two weeks past, she had been wearing gowns hastily sewn for her in wool or linen by village seamstresses, for there was no need for her to wear trousers any more. Yet none of those new gowns were as lovely as this one.

The shimmering fabric imported from France was a gift sent from Magdalene, who had insisted in a message that she had far more of the stuff in an assortment of colors than she would ever need, and her newfound friend was welcome to it.

The gown had just been completed an hour ago and rushed to the castle in time for a feast of celebration... for word had come by messenger, too, that King Edward was dead.

His forces pulled back from Carlisle by his son, another Edward, who appeared to have little taste for battle—at least for now.

Aye, the news had brought much rejoicing, and a new task for Aislinn to direct preparations with the chief cook, Montrose, for an elaborate feast that she hoped would be long remembered.

Sorcha had helped her, too. Aislinn had done everything she could to keep the girl busy so as not to succumb to sadness, though there had still been some tearful moments.

One in particular when Aislinn had showed her the embroidered nightgown Jeanne had given her for her wedding night, but which she'd never worn and would store away for Sorcha. Aye, it was only natural that she would grieve for her parents, but Aislinn felt her heart warmed now as she held out her hand and Sorcha readily took it.

"You look so lovely, Aislinn."

"Ah, sweeting, no more than you," she murmured, for indeed, Sorcha was a truly beautiful girl.

Her braided hair the color of sunlight, her eyes so blue and matching the color of her own silk tunic, her skin as fair as fresh cream, aye, she looked like a Norse princess... which made Aislinn think of what poor Jeanne had told her and Cameron about finding Sorcha as a wee babe. She and Cameron had decided quietly between themselves not to ask questions about what mayhap had no answers, Sorcha's kinsmen, whoever they had been, most likely lost to the sea.

She was their daughter now, through and through, Aislinn drawing her into her arms to give her a big hug.

"Did you decide upon a name for your new rooster?"

"Aye, Speckles," Sorcha said simply, Aislinn not surprised at her choice, for the young bird looked much like the one Sorcha had lost. "He's nicer, though. The old Speckles used tae peck at me."

Aislinn laughed, which made Sorcha laugh, too, as

they walked together from the sumptuous bedchamber that Aislinn shared with Cameron.

She took a last glance over her shoulder at the huge four-poster bed that they had made good use of since returning to the fortress—and she wasn't thinking of sleep.

A delicious shiver coursed through Aislinn as she thought of the impassioned lovemaking that filled their nights and their early mornings and whenever they could sneak away together during the day. Saints in heaven, a few weeks more and she would know for sure if Sorcha had a baby brother or sister due by next winter—aye, she couldn't wait!

Aislinn fairly skipped down the tower steps with Sorcha, her heart felt so light. The boisterous merriment emanating from the great hall grew louder as they drew closer, Cameron's rich laughter rising above the rest.

The sound thrilled her... the scowling warrior she'd first encountered who had been plagued with so distressing an affliction, now her beloved husband, cured by love.

She saw him seated at the head table just as Cameron saw her, too. He rose to stride toward them, looking magnificent in a dark gray tunic with a green and blue breacan—though Sorcha let go of Aislinn's hand and skittered past him to where Daran sat next to Conall.

"The lass has eyes only for your brother," Cameron said as he reached Aislinn, the admiring way his gaze swept over her making her heart skip a beat. "While I have eyes only for you, my beautiful wife..."

He pulled her into his arms and kissed her right there in front of everyone, which made great cheers resound from all that had gathered—warriors and villagers and servants alike.

Yet he drew away just as suddenly and glanced at the

table where Conall had moved down a seat so Sorcha could sit next to Daran, the girl smiling adoringly at him.

"Och, Aislinn, do you think the two of them one day...?"

"Who can say?" she teased him. "He made her a chicken coop, after all. What girl wouldn't be charmed by such a gift?"

Cameron shook his head, teasing in his voice, too, though he heaved a sigh. "I dinna want tae think of when she'll be old enough tae marry and we've suitors banging at the gates—"

"We won't think of it, not tonight," Aislinn broke in gently, thrilling at the warmth of Cameron's fingers as he took her hand to lead her to their seats. "We'll think instead of all the blessings bestowed upon us— Cameron? Why is Conall looking so glum?"

A short laugh escaped Cameron. "Another messenger arrived an hour past from King Robert, who wants Conall tae return tae Dumbarton straightaway. It appears he has a bride in mind for him, though the letter said little else—"

"*A bride?*" Stunned, Aislinn glanced from Cameron, who grinned as if quite pleased with the news, to Conall, who appeared from his dark scowl that he was anything but delighted.

"Aye, what else but a wife tae cure him of *his* affliction?" Cameron whispered against her ear, nuzzling her. "Aislinn Eleanor Campbell... the most precious blessing God could have ever bestowed upon me. My heart... my life."

She hardly heard the roars of approval as Cameron once again swept her into his arms, her cherished husband... his kiss so filled with love... the greatest blessing she had ever known.

ALSO BY MIRIAM MINGER

*Romance from sweet to sensual and historical to contemporary, you're
sure to find stories to love!*

Warriors of the Highlands

My Highland Warrior

My Highland Protector

My Highland Captor

THE MAN OF MY DREAMS

Regency Historical Romance

Secrets of Midnight

My Runaway Heart

My Forbidden Duchess

Kissed At Twilight

My Fugitive Prince

THE O'BYRNE BRIDES

Irish Medieval Historical Romance

Wild Angel

Wild Roses

Wild Moonlight

On A Wild Winter's Night

CAPTIVE BRIDES

Medieval Historical Romance

Twin Passions

Captive Rose

The Pagan's Prize

DANGEROUS MASQUERADE

18th Century Historical Romance

The Brigand Bride

The Scandalous Bride

The Impostor Bride

ROMANTIC SUSPENSE

Operation Hero

INSPIRATIONAL ROMANTIC SUSPENSE

Operation Rescue

TO LOVE A BILLIONAIRE

Steamy Contemporary Romance with an Historical Romance Story within a Story

The Maiden and the Billionaire

The Governess and the Billionaire

The Pirate Queen and the Billionaire

The Highland Bride and the Billionaire

WALKER CREEK BRIDES

Sweet Western Historical Romance

Kari

Ingrid

Lily

Pearl

Sage

Anita

ABOUT THE AUTHOR

Miriam Minger is the bestselling author of sweet to sensual historical romance that sweeps you from Viking times to Regency England to the American West. Miriam is also the author of contemporary romance, romantic suspense, inspirational romance, and children's books. She is the winner of several Romantic Times Reviewer's Choice Awards—including Best Medieval Historical Romance of the Year for The Pagan's Prize—and a two-time RITA Award Finalist for The Brigand Bride and Captive Rose.

Miriam loves to create stories that make you live and breathe the adventure, laugh and cry, and that touch your heart.

For a complete listing of books as well as excerpts and news about upcoming releases, and to connect with Miriam:

Visit Miriam's Website
Subscribe to Miriam's Newsletter